THE
INDIAN MARBLE

George Godfrey

Nishnabek Publications
Athens, Illinois

Nishnabek Publications
24108 Burr Oaks Lane, Athens, Illinois, USA
e-mail: pnginnthewoods@gmail.com

Cover design by Ticara Turley
Cover photograph by E. D. Cashatt

ISBN 978-1494781828

Printed in the United States of America

In Memory

of

Johnie Bergeron

Uncle and Friend

Contents

Acknowledgments

During the time my mother, Helen (Bergeron) Godfrey, and my uncle, Johnie Bergeron, were alive, they provided illustrative information about their grandfather, John (Bat) Baptiste Bergeron, and the family life of William O. and Maude C. Bergeron. Additional insightful material came from my aunts, Alice (Bergeron) Greenwalt and Edith (Bergeron) Wash. My daughter, Cheree Zarbock, had additional information about Bat as told to her by her grandmother. Donna (Lewis) Moody provided information regarding Matilda Lewis. I am grateful to the late Elmer Tabor for the stories that he shared with me about Frank Bazhaw and to the Hampton University Archives for letting me examine Frank's student records. The Cloud County Historical Society (Kansas) provided me with a settler's diary in which John B. Bergeron is mentioned. Jon Boursaw, Legislative Representative, District 4, Citizen Potawatomi Nation, quickly answered a question about the Battle of Dove Creek. White's Residential and Family Services (formerly White's Indiana Manual Labor Institute) sent me information about its educational program of the late 1800's for American Indians. In a variety of ways, the Citizen Potawatomi Nation Cultural Heritage Center rendered assistance. The editorial expertise of Shirley Willard, Rochester, Indiana, corrected my numerous errors in punctuation and spelling in an early draft of this book. My photograph on the back cover is the excellent work of Susan Hoogstraten who allowed me to use the picture. The Illinois State Museum provided literary and technological assistance. Finally, I offer my love and gratitude to my faithful wife, Pat, for her advice, suggestions, and knowledge of child behavior.

Foreword

The Indian Marble stems from the time I was sitting in the living room of my uncle, Johnie Bergeron, who now is deceased. Yearly in June, I go to Shawnee, Oklahoma, for the Citizen Potawatomi Nation's Family Reunion Festival. My visits to Uncle Johnie's farm east of Shawnee also were annual events until his accidental death.

During my sojourns to see Uncle Johnie, our family history always became the subject of our discussion. In the midst of one visit, Uncle Johnie slowly arose from his lounge chair situated in the corner of his living room and disappeared.

He soon returned, holding something in his cupped hands. "I want you to have this," he said in his distinctive way of speaking. "In 1938, I found this on the home site where Bat lived with Madeline Denton." He then opened his hands. In the palm of his right hand was the 1-3/8" brown clay marble pictured on this book's front cover.

Little is known about the history of John B. Bergeron or Bat as he was called. There is some information about him in *Watchekee (Overseer) Walking in Two Cultures,* which I wrote about his mother. Knowledge of his life after he moved to the Citizen Potawatomi Reservation in the Indian Territory is fragmentary: family stories, entries in the 1887 Tribal Roll and an 1891 diary in Kansas, affidavits, and the certificate of his death.

The following fictional history of Bat is an attempt to weave imaginary scenes around known facts and present them in a way that possibly shows what happened to him between his disappearance from the Reservation in the early 1870's and his reappearance in the early 1890's.

Prologue

The first members of the Citizen Potawatomi who moved from northeastern Kansas to the new Reservation in central Indian Territory, now the heart of Oklahoma, faced many obstacles. John (Bat) Baptiste Bergeron was among the first to make this journey. The summer heat and hordes of malaria-carrying mosquitoes and biting horse flies were only the starter problems for him and the others who came.

Bat survived the physical afflictions caused by the weather and insects, but suffered from personal, familial, and societal problems. He partially overcame some of these issues, but a total resolution to them seemed to have escaped and plagued him for the duration of his life.

His methods of dealing with issues closest to him never will be understood. They seem to have been very private and guarded. Regardless, they had lasting effects on his sons, Frank and Will, both negative and positive.

1 – We've Got Guests!

John Pickering commonly encountered skinks and various snakes plus an occasional horny toad on his way to work. While at work he often saw something else, namely Indian children on the porch of his office. So, he was not concerned when he saw two toddler boys quietly sitting alone on a blanket on the porch outside his office.

He recently had started working at the Shawnee Agency in central Indian Territory. Although he commonly was called the Indian Agent, his official title was Superintendent. In his new position, he oversaw the affairs of the Potawatomi and two other Indian tribes, the Absentee Shawnee and the Sac and Fox.[1]

It was late June 1874 when he stepped out of his office to get some relief from the build-up of the afternoon heat that he nearly stumbled over the two boys. With a casual glance, John judged them to be brothers. While quickly sensing that the front porch was not much cooler than his office but at least not stifling, John thought about the two boys and muttered, "The smaller one can't be but two – the other guy can't be much older, perhaps three." The younger one was babbling and fidgeting. John could not help but notice that the older boy stared straight ahead and had his arm wrapped around his brother as if protecting him.

John neither knew the boys' names nor their tribe. He mused to himself, "*They could be Potawatomi, Shawnee, or Sac and Fox.*" Yet, he didn't show any special concern at seeing the young children as he stepped back into his office, He assumed their parents were somewhere at the Agency taking care of business. In the short time that he had been

---

[1]The Kickapoo Reservation was established in 1883.

working at his job with the Indian Department, he had learned that parents often placed their young children on the front porch of his office when they came to the Agency. Thus, it was not unusual for the boys to be by themselves.

The porch offered some shade and what better place to leave children than in the safety of the main building on the Agency grounds. Also, the children had been taught to stay put and not to wander off.

John's biggest concern today was preparing to meet another one hundred or more Potawatomi who were coming from Kansas to relocate on the new Potawatomi Reservation that lay between the North and South Canadian rivers west of the Seminole Reservation. It was important to get the names of the new people and make certain that each member in the new influx of Potawatomi had a sufficient amount of commodity food and enough basic supplies to help them get settled.

******

Taking the office door key out of his pocket, John started to leave his office in late afternoon at the close of the day's work. *"One hundred and twenty-three more people came,"* he recalled. He glanced upward at the still blazing summer sun and momentarily heard the buzzing sounds of the annual cicadas and a katydid chorus. Suddenly, his move to lock the front door was interrupted. The young boys who he had seen around mid-afternoon were still sitting on their blanket, and their parents were nowhere to be seen.

John kept looking at the boys as he locked the door. Placing the door key back in his pocket, he turned and knelt down to talk to the boys. They scarcely looked at him. What John did see was a mix of innocence and bewilderment.

Thinking that the boys must be thirsty, John unlocked his office door and went back inside. He knew that there still was some water in his water bucket. Taking the bucket outside, he again knelt down beside the boys. He tipped the bucket sideways and scooped up a ladle of water. As soon

2

the ladle touched the mouth of the younger boy, he gulped and gurgled. His hands grabbed the ladle, spilling some of the water. Silently, the older boy watched and patiently waited his turn.

He looked into the face of the older boy and asked in English, "What's yer name?"

What John got in return was silence, but the boy's misty eyes told him that the boy was scared. John began wondering if the young children had been abandoned.

Unbeknownst to John, Bat, the boys' father, quietly had left his sons on the porch of the agent's office building several hours earlier before vanishing.

John was uncertain as to what he should do. Finally, he picked up the boys and started home. Speaking softly and in a reassuring voice to the boys, John said, "Molly, my wife, will take good care of you. You can stay with us tonight and tomorrow we'll decide what to do – if need be." Just as he spoke, John caught the unmistakable odor of soiled pants. "Yep," he said as he juggled the boys in his arms to keep them from falling, "Molly will take good care of you!"

Walking into his red sandstone house, John hollered, "MOLLY! We've got guests!"

Looking backward and up from the baking powder biscuits that she was stamping out with a glass on a small table next to her wood-burning stove, Molly saw the boys that John was holding and exclaimed, "Oh, my goodness! Who are they!?" As if trying to look behind John and as her motherly instincts began to mount, she asked, "Where're their parents?"

Much of her concern stemmed from the loss of her only child a mere three months earlier. The child, an infant, had succumbed to whopping cough after getting drenched in a spring rain.

"I don't know the boys' names and know nothing 'bout their mother or father," answered John. "Also, I don't know when their parents are comin' back– considerin' it's gettin' late. Although, I figure they're around and will come

3

Godfrey   *The Indian Marble*

lookin' for their children. Most likely, the first place they'll come lookin' for `em is our place."

"You're probably right'" replied Molly. "When they come, ask `em to stay and eat `fore headin' home."

Because of what John smelled when he picked up the boys, he was careful not to jostle them too hard on his knees after sitting down at the kitchen table. Not looking at Molly but at the boys who he was holding, he said, "First, we'd better wash these guys' hands! The younger one might need his bottom cleaned. Phew!" Looking into the youngster's brown eyes, John said, "You stink!".

"Supper's ready," said Molly as she put the last fork on the table. "Any attention for the boys can wait."

In spite of the younger boy's aroma, John was able to eat heartily. After a burping when he was finished eating, John turned to his wife and said, "Molly, wash up the boys really good before puttin' `em to bed. They need a good scrubbin'."

After fetching water enough and warming it up before pouring it into a large copper tub, Molly began taking off the boys' clothing. It took some insistence before the older boy would let her take off his shirt. As she did, a scrap of paper fell out with a message on it. Molly carefully read the note that was written on it.

"JOHN! Come read this note! I found it inside the older boy's shirt!"

2 – Pond Creek Flood

When Bat crossed the North Canadian River, he felt he was out of danger. His horse, Buck, a buckskin gelding, was winded and lathered from having been ridden hard. Even though Bat was safe, he did not know what would happen to his sons who were only two miles away. The thought of them kept recycling in his mind, *"What will happen to them?"*

Bat rode a bit farther and finally made camp. He settled down for the night north of the Shawnee village that was along the North Canadian River, the northern boundary of the recently created Citizen Potawatomi Reservation. The image that he witnessed earlier in the day repeatedly flashed through Bat's mind. He shuddered at the thought of what could have happened to him.

******

Bat had come down from the Potawatomi Reservation in northeastern Kansas only two years earlier. The move to the new reservation in the Indian Territory was to have given him a fresh start – new land – a place to start his own cattle herd – a quiet place to live and raise a family.

His parents, Francis Bergeron and Watchekee, had come down from Kansas at the same time. They helped him start his herd. However, his mother died shortly after her arrival. Her death was triggered when she came to the defense of Bat's father when he was being roughed up by two drifters. One had roped Francis and was dragging him through a mud puddle not far from his cabin. His mother saved Francis but killed and scalped the drifter. Her action was viewed as scandalous by the U. S. Marshal who lived on the Choctaw Reservation and now was responsible for enforcing federal law on the Citizen Potawatomi Reservation.

Bat was left alone, emotionally and distraught, over the death of his mother, Watchekee, and in the business-sense after his father, Francis, moved back to Wamego, Kansas. His father still owned a house in Wamego and strongly voiced that he wanted to go back to it rather than continue living on the new reservation in Indian Territory without the comfort and companionship of his Potawatomi wife. Their relationship of thirty-two years tracked back to Illinois, the state where Bat had been baptized.

******

Other tragic happenings crossed Bat's mind beside the one that he had endured only hours ago. He now lay awake. The din of the snowy tree cricket and katydid sounds in the trees overhead went ignored. Even the call of the whip-poor-will, which he usually enjoyed hearing went unheard. The piercing scream of a bobcat around midnight scarcely was noticed by him. Uppermost in his mind were thoughts that kept recycling in his mind: *"Why did I ever bring my family down here from Kansas? – Mary – What'll happen to Frank and Will? – I had to run or get lynched."*

Bat, his wife, Mary, and their two sons, Frank and Will, started their lives on the Citizen Potawatomi Reservation in a dugout; but he promised Mary that he would build her a cabin near Little River. Bat and Mary carved their dugout out of the red clay, which typified the whole reservation. It was not far east of the two-room log cabin where Bat's sister, Kate Melot, lived with her husband, Joe, along with their growing family. Both abodes faced southward, overlooking the beauty of Pond Creek Valley with its abundant, swaying prairie grasses.

The beauty of the valley did not extend to the dugout. It only brought a degree of shelter to Bat and his family. Though the hills overlooking the dugout were dotted with many juniper and scrub oak trees, they brought little comfort to those in the log cabin and even less to Bat and Mary in the dugout.

The cabin and the dugout offered shade and protection from the horse flies but not from the swarms of mosquitoes. Several of the Potawatomi, who had traveled with the group that Bat was with, contracted malaria.

Joe Melot tried to protect his horses from the myriad of biting flies by tying his horses together and having them stand in smoke. Neither the intense heat of the area nor the quinine from nearby Paul's Valley nor the smoke could abate the mosquitoes that brought misery to the people.

One afternoon when Bat was helping Joe set a smoky fire, Mary clutched her stomach and screamed. By the time Bat reached her, Mary lay on the ground shaking and in immense pain.

Following right after Bat, who had picked up his wife in his sweaty arms, Joe said, "Take her to my cabin!" Kate already knew Mary was pregnant and always had trouble birthing. Thus, she realized the seriousness of situation when she heard Mary scream and saw Bat carrying her to the cabin. Waiting in front of her cabin, Kate directed Bat to put Mary on the bed. "Hurry!" she exclaimed.

Sitting on a stool in the cabin's 'dog trot' after getting Mary inside, Bat turned to his brother-in-law, looked up, and said, "She'll be alright. She's a strong woman."

Several hours went by. Stillness often was punctuated by Mary's cries of agony. Then, there was silence – no cries of agony – not even the sound of a squalling baby. The silence made Bat and Joe nervously look at each other. Slowly Kate opened the door and stood in the doorway. Bat apprehensively stood up and stared at his sister. Kate's tear-stained face immediately told him that something was wrong. Looking directly at Bat, Kate said in a soft mournful voice, "Mary's gone – the babies too."

"Mary's dead?" replied Bat in a disbelieving voice. "You said babies. Whadda you mean babies?"

"She tried to have twins," answered Kate as she put her arms around Bat in an effort to console him.

Bat pushed Kate aside and went into the bedroom. Mary' lifeless body lay on the bed with her dead twins covered with a bloody blanket.

Kate and Joe heard but a few sobs. After a few minutes, a stoic Bat appeared in the doorway and said, "She always liked the creek." He cast his eyes in the direction of Pond Creek. "I expect we should bury her and the babies down there." He scarcely waved his arm toward the creek as he slumped to the floor. Joe didn't know what to say.

Suddenly, Bat stood up. "Frank and Will are alone in the dugout!" He started to get up and go to his sons, but Kate intervened and said, "You stay here. I'll go get the boys."

Joe managed to build a wooden coffin into which he placed both Mary and the twins. The burial was simple and was attended by the Potawatomi who lived nearby in dugouts similar to Bat's. No priests or protestant ministers conducted the service because there were no clergy in the area.

As nightfall came, Bat looked at his sons, Frank and Will, who were balled together in deep slumber. His sons were oblivious of their mother's death. In the dark dugout illuminated by a single kerosene lamp on the kitchen table, Bat pulled a blanket over them and quietly said, "Mama's gone – but I'll take care of you."

Just as Bat extinguished the flame of the lamp there was a flash from a nearby lightning strike almost immediately followed by a very loud BOOM. Bat peered out the dugout's door and thought, *"That was close!"*

A late spring thunder storm was passing through the Pond Creek Valley. Throughout much of the night, lightning flashes followed by crashes of thunder, violent winds, and heavy rain raged. Before long, Pond Creek began to roil. As it left its banks, large chunks of the red soil were loosened and washed away.

Dawn broke with blue sky and peaceful, puffy clouds lazily drifting by. Pond Creek was heavily laden with red silt. The old banks seemingly had been swallowed, and new banks had been sculptured by the night's flood water. At least, the stream no longer was at flood stage, but its current was swift and filled with floating tree trunks

Bat emerged from his dugout. Seeing that his sister was up and looking at her garden, he shouted, "Kate! Mind watching Frank and Will for about an hour? I want to go down to Mary's grave."

Kate, barefoot, pulled her corn cob pipe out of her mouth, and yelled back, "Glad to help! Be right over! The garden is too wet to do anythin' with it!"

She put on her moccasins and ventured over to where Bat was standing in front of his dugout. Together, with her arm around Bat's waist, they went inside his dugout. She aroused the boys and took them to her cabin so they could eat breakfast.

Seeing that Frank and Will were in the hands of his sister, Bat saddled his horse and rode down to where Mary was buried. He was shocked to see that her grave had vanished. Instead, there was only a new, water-soaked bank and foaming water that raced below the point where he remained astride his horse. After but a few minutes, he sadly reined his horse around and silently rode back to Kate's cabin to get his sons.

3 – The Lynching

"Let's get the horses. We'll bring 'em in and tie 'em in the smoke. The horse flies are starting to bite," said Joe to Bat. Together with Bat and another neighbor, Benjamin Tescier, Joe strolled out to the prairie to round up his horses. Bat and Benjamin already had brought in theirs.

"How about that!" exclaimed Joe. "Belle had her colt last night!"

The three men trained their eyes on Joe's sorrel mare. Standing next to her was a spindly-legged pinto colt.

Bat suddenly halted. "What's wrong?" asked Benjamin. In a hushed voice, Bat said, "Look at Belle. She's guardin' her colt – her ears are laid back. None of the other horses are grazin'. They're lookin' at that small clump of trees off to their right."

Joe then saw a slight movement in the clump of trees. "I see what's got 'em spooked," he said quietly. As he spoke, he raised his rifle and shot. POW! A mountain lion flipped into the air and fell lifeless to the ground. It had been stalking the horses in hopes of bringing down the new foal.

After the men got the horses calmed down and haltered, they led them to where Kate already had started a smoky fire. On the way back, Joe commented to Bat, "What you gonna do now? You lost your mother last year and Mary two months ago. Besides that your father, Francis, has gone back to Kansas."

"Finish my cabin up by Little River," replied Bat. "Mary would want me to."

"You're 'bout done with it – right?" inquired Joe.

Bat momentarily stopped and said, "Yeah – nothin' but some of the shingles left to do. The hard work's already

10

done. Wish the shinglin' had been done `fore Mary died. I'm goin' up there tomorrow to work on it."

"Want some help?" asked Joe and Benjamin almost simultaneously.

"Thanks, but I need to go up there myself. Well, almost by myself. I'm takin' Frank and Will with me. John Whitehead and Mrs. Whitehead don't live too far north of where I'll be. I'll ask John's wife to watch the boys while I'm workin'."

******

Early the next morning, Bat mounted Buck, his two year-old buckskin gelding, after preparing for the ride to his cabin near Little River and gathering tools for the work which lay ahead of him. A second horse, a sorrel mare, carried his tools as well as the food and supplies that he and the boys would need for camping. He knew that it would be a two-day trip to Whitehead's cabin. With two young boys, the trip would be slow. The first day would just be riding followed by camping for the night.

Bat figured that he would have to pass by his cabin early the next morning, take Frank and Will up to the Whitehead's place so Mrs. Whitehead could watch them, and then double back to his own cabin three miles to the south. Working alone, he planned to finish shingling the south roof of his cabin by early afternoon.

Joe handed Will to Bat and boosted Frank so that he could ride behind the saddle. Joe looked at Frank and said, "Be sure and hold onto your father. By the way, here's your blanket." As Frank grabbed the blanket and pushed it down between him and the seat of the saddle, Bat and Joe gave each other a sly grin.

"Sure you don't want me to come and help?" asked Joe.

"I want to finish the cabin myself," answered Bat. "Like I said yesterday, 'The hard work's done.' Thanks to what we did `fore Mary died, there's a pile of shingles waitin' to be put on the roof." Bat then turned his horse and rode east toward the Arbuckle Wagon Road. The road would take him north to his cabin, which overlooked the valley of Little River. Trailing behind was his pack horse. It walked along with its head extended forward because its lead rope was tied to the tail of the buckskin that Bat was riding.

The procession of three riders on one horse followed by a second horse tied to the one in front of it caused Joe to chuckle. *"It's comical but sad,"* he thought to himself as he watched Bat and his sons disappear beyond the stands of abundant post oak and cedar trees. *"Mary was lookin' forward to movin' out of the dugout and into her own cabin."*

Joe than turned his gaze in the direction of Pond Creek where Mary's body got washed away. After standing motionless for a few minutes, he lowered his head and walked slowly back to his cabin.

******

The melodic sounds of a nearby mocking bird and the morning rays of the sun awakened Bat. After watering and leading the horses to clumps of prairie grasses, Bat started a cooking fire and next roused Frank and Will. Frank helped as much as he could in his three-year-old way while Will, sleepy-eyed, held tightly to the left leg of Bat's trousers. After a breakfast of fried eggs and day-old, somewhat hardened biscuits, the horses were brought back and saddled and loaded. Soon, the trio resumed their trip to see the Whiteheads.

The trek along the Arbuckle Wagon Road took Bat and his sons about one hundred yards west of their unfinished cabin. It was done except for a large, open patch on the south roof. Bat paused for a short while when he saw the cabin and thought, *"I'll get done with the roof today, and we can move in. I wish that Mary could've enjoyed it and the twins could've lived to have grown up in it."*

A few miles after Bat and his boys crossed Little River, Bat began to get glimpses of the Whitehead cabin through the oaks and cedars. The cabin was fifty yards west of the Arbuckle Wagon Road and had a narrow lane leading to it. When Bat reached the cabin, he saw John Whitehead who was in his front yard cinching up the saddle on his horse. A few chickens scurried away when Bat rode in.

"Mornin'," said Bat as he greeted his old friend.

"Mornin'" to you too, Bat. Say, I'm sorry to hear 'bout Mary. See you got Frank and Will with you. The three of you gonna work on your cabin. Gonna finish it today? You've got only a little shinglin' left to do. Want some help? Soon as I find my milk cow, I'll come by."

"Thanks," but I want to work by myself if Abigail can watch the boys today."

"ABIGAIL, come see who stopped by!" yelled John Whitehead.

"No need to yell! I seen Bat comin' and heard what he wants me to do. I'm glad to help. Just hand the boys to me. They'll be just fine."

First, Bat handed Will to Abigail's outstretched hands and then turned in his saddle and helped Frank get down. John had to grab Frank and stand him up to prevent him from falling to the ground. Seeing that his boys were in good hands, Bat set off to work on his cabin's roof.

******

Shortly after the sun reached its midpoint in the sky, Bat satisfied that the shingling was done, started climbing down his rickety ladder. Just as he put his foot in the first rung, he was startled when he heard a voice. Looking down, he saw two men on lathered and panting horses. The man closest to him was shouting to him while the other man with long black haired nervously kept looking toward the Arbuckle Wagon Road.

Both strangers were dark-skinned. Bat thought, *"They look half Indian, like me."*

"Sorry to scare you, but we need water for our horses. Got some? We'll be on our way then. We want to get to and

head west on the Cheyenne . . . what's it called?" asked
Anthony, the man on a lathered-up bay.

"Cheyenne Agency Wagon Road from what I
remember," answered the second man, Bert, who kept
looking in the direction of the Arbuckle Wagon Road.

"I just finished my roof when I heard you holler. I
was comin' down and on my way to get my own horse. He's
the buckskin over under that there tree. – I need to water him
too and then be headin' north to get my boys. You're
welcome to follow me. We can water the horses at Little
River along the way. It's not far from here. A short distance
beyond where we'll water the horses is the wagon road that
will take you to the Cheyenne Agency. I'll take you to the
road as soon as I get my horse saddled."

The men were anxious to leave, but didn't want Bat
to become suspicious. They, therefore, acted patient and
were courteous to him as he climbed down the ladder and
went to saddle up Buck.

Bat was content to walk Buck to Little River, but the
man who had shouted to Bat as he was climbing down from
the cabin roof curtly said, "We're kinda in a hurry. Mind if
we gallop?"

"No problem," replied Bat. "Besides my boys
probably are gettin' anxious to see me." At the same time,
Bat thought, *"These guys seem to want to get somewhere fast.
I hope their horses last to where ever they're goin'. They've
been ridden hard by the looks of them bein' all lathered up
and winded."*

The trio reached Little River in only a few minutes.
There the two strangers' horses and Bat's quenched their
thirst.

"By the looks of your horses, I wouldn't let them
drink too much – especially if you still got some hard ridin'
ahead of you," commented Bat. "I only gotta . . ."

Before Bat could finish his sentence, a five-man
posse galloped up and surrounded Bat and the two strangers.
Seeing that the posse had their guns trained on them, the two

men on winded horses took their hands away from their holstered pistols.

"Didn't know there were three of you," graveled Ed Trumball, the U.S. Marshal who was in charge of the posse.

"Three? Three of what?" nervously asked Bat.

"Shut up! You know what we do to horse thieves in these parts."

Bat became defensive and said, "Horse thieves! I don't even know these two."

"I said 'Shut up!'" firmly said Ed.

"Wait a minute!" interrupted Chet. "Me and Albert know this man. You're Bat – Bat Bergeron – right? Look, Ed, his horse isn't lathered up. He wasn't ridin' with the other two."

Bat became a little relaxed when Chet intervened, but was upset at what Ed said next. "A Bergeron, huh? – Didn't steal your horse, huh? How come you Bergerons are always causin' me problems? Was your mother, Josette?"

"Yes."

"That figures! I came up to investigate her killin' and scalpin' a man. It probably was a good thing she died before I got a chance to talk to her!"

"He's not one of us!" blurted Anthony.

Bert started to agree, but Ed struck him on the side of the head with his pistol. Then Ed jerked his horse around so he was facing Bat and firmly said, "YOU GET OUT OF HERE AND DON'T COME BACK FOR SEVEN YEARS! I mean the whole area!"

"Wait!" implored Bat.

"You heard me! I'm givin' you a chance to get out of here unless you want your neck stretched! Before you leave you're gonna watch – wanna give you something to help you remember!"

Ed cocked his revolver and aimed it at Bat's right temple. Sweat profusely ran down Bat's forehead as nooses were put around the necks of the strangers who already were bound with their hands behind their backs. The other ends of the ropes were thrown over stout tree branches. Bat winced as the horses bearing the men were swatted, and the men were jerked off their saddles by short ropes. The men dropped. They swung like pendulums for a few moments.

Because the hanging ropes were short, the men slowly were strangled. Longer ropes would have broken their necks, and their death would have been quicker. Finally, their feet twitched and all movement stopped. The two horse thieves dangled from the hanging ropes just a few feet in front of Bat.

"Now, get out of here!" yelled Ed to Bat.

Bat turned to Chet and anxiously pleaded, "My boys are not far from here! I need to get them!"

Chet and Albert quickly spoke to Ed in hushed tones.

Lifting his head, Ed stared at Bat and said, "Chet and Albert will ride with you. Remember, seven years!"

Shocked by what had just happened, Bat looked over his shoulder as he rode his horse into Little River before dashing across to the opposite bank. What he saw were two hung men – a sickening sight that was seared into his memory.

Hastily, Bat, guarded by Chet and Albert, rode north to John's cabin.

Frank and Will were sound asleep in the shade of a large pecan tree when Bat rode in flanked by Chet and Albert. Abigail saw the men coming and strolled out of her cabin to offer them a drink of water. She was taken back when the water was refused.

John, pulling up his suspenders, came out of his cabin behind Abigail. When Bat saw him he yelled, "John! Help the boys onto my horse! Put Will in front of me on the saddle and Frank behind me. Don't have time to explain! Throw me Frank's blanket and bring me the pack horse. I'll need the supplies on her!"

John and Abigail were flabbergasted at Bat's behavior, the look on his face, and his not introducing what they thought were his friends.

When the boys were well-seated, Bat, hanging onto the lead of the pack horse, neck-reined his horse around and left. John, although squinting because of near-sightedness, could tell that Bat turned and rode north. John turned to his wife and said, "That's strange. Bat lives south of us – near Rock Springs where his mother and father used to live."

Seeing that Bat fled north after getting his boys, Chet and Albert stopped, turned around, and rode south where they soon joined the other members of the posse.

The scene that Bat had fled had become surreal by the time Chet and Albert returned. The other members of the posse were laughing. Almost cavalier-like, they rolled and offered cigarettes to Chet and Albert as they trotted into the lynching scene.

Finally, Ed rather quietly grumbled as he nudged his horse forward, "We got 'em. Alex, cut 'em down. Let's go home. Albert, grab the reins of the horses they tried to steal."

Slowly, the posse started trotting their horses south on the Arbuckle Wagon Road toward the Choctaw Reservation.

4 – It's Too Dangerous

Bat galloped his horses north to Shawneetown after leaving the Whitehead's. Because of the speed and jostling of the horse, it was difficult for Bat to keep Frank and Will from falling off his horse. He had to hold Will tightly and kept telling Frank to hang on. Bat feared for his own life as he raced along.

He wanted to take his sons with him after he got off the Citizen Potawatomi Reservation, but he began thinking that his boys were too young for him to take them with him – wherever that would be.

When Bat got to the south edge of Shawneetown, he reined Buck to a halt and jumped to the ground taking care not to knock Frank and Will off the heavily breathing Buck. There, he fumbled through his saddle bags and found a stubby pencil and a wrinkled piece of paper. Thankful that he learned to read and write at St. Mary's Mission in Kansas, he quickly scrawled a note. It read: "Frank's the bigger one. His little brother is Will. Please take them to Kate Melot. Had to leave in a hurry." It was signed, "Bat Bergeron." He then tucked the note inside the front of Frank's shirt and climbed back onto his horse.

He walked his horses the rest of the way into Shawneetown so as not to bring attention to himself. Upon reaching the Indian Agent's office, he looked around to see that no one was looking. Satisfied that he was not being watched, he spread out Frank's blanket and placed Frank and Will on it. Not knowing how to say good-bye to his sons because he was not sure that he would ever see them again, he quickly mounted Buck and fled the Citizen Potawatomi Reservation.

Once across the North Canadian River, he entered the Sac and Fox Indian Reservation and began to feel safe from the posse. He was safe but in emotional turmoil because he had left his sons behind. Bat had been a respected Potawatomi man with a bright future before him. Now, he was a loner. In his mind, he was a drifter who had abandoned his sons.

****

Bat finally broke camp at the first rays of dawn after his fitful night north of Shawneetown. After eating the boiled eggs he originally had planned for breakfast for himself and the boys on their way back to their dugout, he laid out the other things he had put in the bags being carried by his pack horse. There wasn't much, only a few dried biscuits, some jerky, and two more boiled eggs. He had planned to hunt for meat to supplement what he had brought. Now the latter was not possible because the U.S, Marshal in the posse had taken his guns away. *"Somehow,"* he thought, *"I'll have to get more supplies. How? I've only got thirty-seven cents and no way to shoot somethin' to eat."*

In a despondent mood, Bat began riding north on the West Shawnee Trail. Throughout the morning, he hung his head half-asleep as his horses slowly plodded northward. The slow cadence allowed him to doze and catch up on sleep that had escaped him during the night.

Shortly before noon day, Bat spotted a large patch of blackberries. The patch bordered the dense woods of Cross Timbers, a wood land of oaks and cedar underlain by nearly impenetrable underbrush that stretched from central Texas to southeastern Kansas. The trail that Bat was on, allowed him to pass through the thick maze of vegetation. Near the blackberries was a meadow of prairie grass and a small stream. Seeing the clearing brought him some sense of relief and caused him to say to his buckskin, "We'll take a rest, and all of us can eat."

The stream provided Bat and his horses the water they needed. Afterward, Bat led Buck and the pack horse to the prairie, hobbled them, and turned them loose to graze. Then he started plucking off the ripe blackberries and eating them. The ripe fruit was so abundant that Bat soon got his fill. Thinking ahead, he started collecting blackberries in his hat so he would have some when he stopped for the night.

The jingling sound of moving wagons broke the silence and solitude of Bat's location. However, a turn in the trail prevented him from seeing who was coming. Considering his predicament, Bat didn't care. He was focused on filling his hat with the blackberries. To him, the blackberries were more important than the sound of the moving wagons, a sound that got louder as the wagons approached him.

"Well I'll be!" exclaimed the voice. "BAT!"

Bat had his back to the trail when he heard the loud call his name. He jerked and turned around in the direction of the voice. To his amazement, the people that he saw were Citizen Potawatomi who had left Kansas and were moving to their new reservation in Indian Territory. Bat recognized all of them, but he was speechless.

The group was led by Joseph LaFromboise, one of the Potawatomi chiefs. Sitting next to him in his wagon was his wife. Just then, the smiling face of Joseph's daughter, Madeline, popped out of the wagon and appeared over Joseph's shoulder.

After a very brief moment of staring and silence, Joseph tied his team's reins around the wagon brake handle and climbed down. What usually was a soft handshake turned into an emotional embrace, especially on Bat's part.

"How'd you come down?" asked Bat.

"We decided to stay on the east side of the Flint Hills rather than take the Chisholm Trail. Some of our group wanted to see where their parents lived in eastern Kansas after their long walk from Indiana.[2]   Also, Jeb, over there, was stationed in Fort Row in southeastern Kansas during the Civil War. He said there was a decent wagon road that would take us past the fort and into the Indian Territory. He also told us about the trail we're on now," said Joseph.

"I know about Fort Row," said Bat. "Archange, my sister – anyway her husband, Mok-je-win, was there too. Part of the reason why our reservation is near here is because of what Joe, my sister Kate's husband, heard from Mok-je-win."

"Our biggest problem was getting across the Arkansas River in Cherokee country – all of us had to be ferried.   Once we got past it, we got on this here West Shawnee Trail." Joseph stomped his boot on a dry wagon rut and raised a small cloud of reddish dust and continued, "This is the trail that Jeb talked about. According to this here map, we should be close to our new Reservation, but we have to ford the North Canadian River first.   How far is it from here?" Without giving Bat a chance to answer his question, Joseph asked him about his family. "Say, how's Mary and the boys?"

The look on Bat's face immediately told Joseph that something was wrong.

Bat stared straight ahead as he quietly talked. "Mary died two months ago."

"Sorry to hear that," said Joseph as he turned and looked upward as a form of expressing sympathy.

Joseph turned around and faced the wagon train behind him. "PULL INTO THE PRAIRIE! WE'LL REST AND EAT! UNHITCH YOUR TEAMS!" he commanded. Pointing, he shouted, "WATER 'EM IN THE STREAM OVER THERE!"

"Let's go and sit in the shade where we can talk," said Joseph as he put his arm around Bat and led him to a nearby tree where they sat down.

---

[2] The 'long walk' is now known as 1838 Tail of Death.

Once the two men were comfortably seated, Bat continued, "Yesterday, I went to finish my cabin and ended up getting accused of stealin' my horse and being ordered to leave the area for seven years – nearly got hung. Because I'm on the run, I had to leave the boys on the Indian Agent's porch – felt that it wouldn't be good on them to run with me."

"What?" Joseph replied in disbelief. "Want to go back? I'll be glad to vouch for you."

Almost instantly, the image of seeing the twitching feet of the lynched men flashed through Bat's mind. Bat replied, "Thanks. But it's too dangerous. Best if I keep goin'."

"What you gonna do? Where you headed?" asked Joseph.

"Don't know," answered Bat. "Barely got any money, and my guns got taken away – can't even shoot anythin' to eat. Don't know where I'll go or what'll I do."

Bat's response was followed by several minutes during which neither man spoke. Their silence was broken only by the squeals of the children who had jumped and climbed out of the wagons. They were happily running and playing. Overhead, a fox squirrel chatted its alarm call when it spotted a bull snake lounging on a tree stump.

Joseph cast his eyes in the direction of Bat's horses. Pondering he inquired, "Are you taking both horses with you? Sure you need both of them?"

"The mare? She's my pack horse."

"Why do you need a pack horse? If I was by myself, I'd take everything I need with me on one horse."

Bat began to understand what Joseph was getting at and said, "When I took Frank and Will with me to finish my cabin, I needed to take food and campin' gear. I needed the pack horse to carry it. Guess that I was thinkin' of the food still in the packs when I grabbed her and ran. Why'd you ask? Want to buy the mare"

"Perhaps," answered Joseph. "You mentioned a cabin. Is it done?"

"Yes. I just got the shingles put on it when the actual horse thieves came along. Everything's done except for diggin' the well and the pit for the outhouse."

Joseph got up and strolled over to his wagon. He reached into it and picked up his spare revolver and rifle. After grabbing a handful of bullets for each firearm, he returned to where Bat was sitting. Looking down at Bat, he said in a calm voice, "These are yours. Now – let's work out a deal for the pack horse and your cabin."

With Joseph now sitting beside him, Bat picked up the guns. In a heart-felt voice he said "*Mgwetch* (Thanks).

"Don't know where to start on the other things," commented Joseph, "but the way I figure it, the mare's only worth about thirty dollars. I'll buy her . . ."

"I know that I'm in a bad way, but she's worth more than that," responded Bat in a guarded fashion.

"How much you want for her then?"

"I paid seventy, but I'll take fifty."

"Fair enough. You've sold her – I'll buy her," said Joseph grinning.

Turning real estate broker, Joseph said, "I think Jeb over yonder might want your cabin. He got hurt just as we were leaving Kansas and can't work very much – at least for now – and his wife is expecting next month. I'm sure he'll be interested. There won't be any problem in getting others to dig his well and pit. Where'd he get water before the well gets dug is one thing that concerns me – I'm not concerned about the pit now."

"Little River – a short ride from the cabin – is where one can get water," replied Bat. "But I don't want to sell the cabin – at least not right now."

"How come?" asked Joseph. "You told me that you got run off the reservation."

"I got run off for seven years. I hope to come back some day and will need a place to live when I do."

"Do you want to rent it then with the understanding that you can get into your cabin when you return?" pressed Joseph.

"I'm willin' to make that kind of deal."

"How much?" inquired Joseph.

Bat mulled the matter in his head for a few minutes and said, "Sixty-five dollars for seven years."

"Jeb – come over here! Me and Bat want to discuss something with you!"

Jeb hobbled over to where Bat and Joseph were sitting.

Joseph looked up at Jeb and said, "Bat here has a cabin for you, at least one you can rent for several years. Interested?"

"Perhaps. How much and for how long, Bat?"

"Sixty-five dollars for seven years."

"You're very generous. I'd like to accept your offer, but the most I can pay you now is twelve dollars and two bits. I'll pay you the balance later."

"Bat, you told me that you're going to be travelling," said Joseph. "Are you willing to let me get the rest from Jeb and somehow get it to you?"

"You've got a cabin, Jeb," said Bat.

5 – Cross Timbers Struggle

Bat's original intention was to go back to the old reservation in Kansas. He was headed that way until Joseph LaFromboise's group spotted him picking blackberries beside the West Shawnee Trail. He was grateful for the help he got and for the business transactions that he and Joseph made. At the same time, Bat was depressed for having abandoned Frank and Will at the Indian Agent's office.

Joseph gathered his group together for an impromptu council meeting. He opened it by saying, "Bat tells me that our reservation is about eleven miles away. We could get there yet today, but it would be dark by the time we arrive. My suggestion is that we stop and camp here tonight and be on our way early tomorrow morning. We'll get there around noon."

A consensus was reached at the council meeting to wait until tomorrow's dawn before resuming travel. The decision greatly delighted Bat because he had company with people he knew and would get a good meal in the evening and a hearty breakfast in the morning.

******

Dawn stirred the travelers, and after breakfast, Joseph LaFromboise and his group were once again moving south. Bat tipped his hat when Joseph's group of relocating Potawatomi passed by him on its way to the Citizen Potawatomi Reservation. It was his way of saying *ba mi pi* (a loose version of good-bye) and *mgwetch*. He now had two guns and seventy-two dollars and sixty two cents plus a sack of food provisions. The previous day, he nearly had been destitute.

As soon as the group was out of sight, Bat left the West Shawnee Trail and started through Cross Timbers. His goal was to head west, find the Chisholm Trail, and take it south. The plan, in his frame of mind, would accomplish two things: circumvention of the Citizen Potawatomi Reservation in which he had been threatened with lynching and avoiding having to explain and justify his child abandonment to his relatives and friends still on the old reservation in Kansas.

Bat knew that a span of prairie lay between the western edge of Cross Timbers and the Chisholm Trail. However, the challenge was to find his way through Cross Timbers. It only was twenty-five miles wide, but, in addition to the thick under bush, the area was littered with dead and snarled limbs that had been ripped from the trees. They were the victims of countless wind and ice storms that had swept through the region during the past decades.

Bat knew the frustration and danger of traveling in a circle when passing through an unfamiliar area. As he began his trek through Cross Timbers, he recalled that the Potawatomi from Indiana on the long walk in 1838 got lost in the prairie region of eastern Kansas and were led in a circle. To avoid the same mistake in the densely vegetated area in which he found himself, Bat relied on his past scouting experiences when he worked at Fort Riley in Kansas. He carefully used *kises* (Grandfather Sun) as his navigational aid to keep him on a westward course.

Buck nimbly picked his way through the tangled under brush. The thickly-wooded vegetation occasionally gave way to glades. When they were encountered, Bat stopped and let Buck graze before moving on. The streams, all tributaries to the North Canadian River, were but few. However, they gave Bat and Buck the refreshing water they needed to trudge ahead. At one point, Bat judged that he soon would be out of the dreaded Cross Timbers. However, when he crested a hill, Bat saw a small canyon with red sandstone walls blocking his passage. Slowly, he led his buckskin down to the canyon's base. A small stream lazily coursed through the canyon.

Kneeling beside his horse, Bat said, "Well Buck, let's get a drink and then find a way to get up the other side."

When both Bat and Buck were drinking, Bat heard an ominous sound. Quickly, he mounted Buck and dashed up the east side of the canyon. He did not have time to consider the easiest route. The innocent stream, from which they had been drinking only moments before, suddenly was transformed into a raging torrent of frothy reddish water. A storm many miles upstream had triggered a flash flood that came roaring through the canyon.

Reaching the safety of the hill, Bat said, "Buck, all we can do is wait for the water to go down. Then, we'll find a way to go up the other side."

After Bat got safely across the canyon, he noticed that the trees and the dead limbs were less dense. "Buck, I think we soon will be out of the Timbers," said Bat. He gently put Buck into a trot hoping to soon find the Chisholm Trail.

Suddenly, Bat pulled Buck's reins and stopped. Before him was a wide swath of mangled and twisted trees that stretched in a diagonal line from the southwest to the northeast. As far southwest as he could see, Bat saw the same path of destruction. *"A tornado recently blew through here,"* thought Bat. He got off Buck to see if the trees were beginning to leaf out. *"By the looks of things, it must've been about two months ago. It probably was the same storm that washed away Mary's grave down at Pond Creek."*

Some of the trees were showing signs of recovery, but the damage was so severe that passage through the downed trees was impossible. He said, "Buck – the only thing we can do is ride southwest until we can head west."

The southwest direction that Bat took led him back to the North Canadian River. Bat thought about what the U.S. Marshal told him, *"YOU GET OUT OF HERE AND DON'T COME BACK FOR SEVEN YEARS!"* The images of the two horse thieves being hung and his being forced to watch

27

caused Bat to shiver. He still feared for his life, but figured that he was far enough west of the Citizen Potawatomi Reservation to be out of danger of being lynched.

Two things struck Bat when he approached the North Canadian. There was no more tornado damage. Suddenly, he recognized where he was at. *"I've gotten to the Chisholm Trail! I can see where it crosses the North Canadian!"* He looked to his left and saw a willow thicket on a sand bar. It was the same willow thicket that concealed him and Pete Anderson to figure out why there was shooting when they were approaching the river in Indian Territory two years ago. It turned out that the drovers were shooting their guns to scare their herd of longhorns across the river.

6 – Avoiding the Marshal

Mead's trading post on the upper bank of the North Canadian River provided Bat a spot to rest from his arduous trek through Cross Timbers. Mead couldn't believe Bat had come that way and figured that Bat must be on the run, but didn't pry.

The second morning after Bat was recuperating, he went into the trading post to buy some supplies. As he entered the cabin-turned store, Mead said, "Say – what'd you 'all say yer name was? Never mind. I just remembered – Bat. Bat, you any good at breaking horses? I got a couple of two year-olds in my corral needin' some good work, especially the flea-bit gray mare.   I like to have some good ridin' horses around.   Never know who might be passin' through and wantin' a second horse – or even a horse."

"I broke Buck last fall. He was tough. How much you payin'?" inquired Bat.

"Fifty cents a head."

"Throw in a rain slicker and you've got a deal."

As the two men shook hands, Bat said, "After I get the horses broke, I'll be movin' on."

"How long it'll take you?"

"One day."

******

Because of his 'horse whisperer' techniques, Bat did not get sore from breaking the two horses. Early the next morning, he started riding south to the Darlington Indian Agency, an outpost that worked with the Arapaho and Cheyenne. His actual destination was the newly established Fort Reno, a few miles west of the agency. Trailing behind him on a lead rope was the flea-bit gray. He successfully had forgone the one dollar for breaking the two horses and the rain slicker in exchange for buying one of the horses for fifty dollars. He knew that a freshly broken mare would bring a much higher price in the right venue.

Immediately upon arriving at Fort Reno, Bat sought out the fort's commandant, Colonel Gerald McComber, to apply as an Indian Scout. He figured that his experience as a scout at Fort Riley in Kansas in the 1860's would be a good talking point. He was right.

Seven months after he started working at Ft. Reno, Bat came in from a scouting expedition that had taken him northwest into Cheyenne country. Bat was tired and cold, but he unsaddled and rubbed down Buck before putting him into the same stall as Lucy, the flea bit-gray mare that he had brought with him from Mead's trading post. Buck quivered when Bat slid off the saddle and bobbed his head up and down in anticipation of the oats that were awaiting him.

Bat started to walk out of the horse barn to get a hot cup of coffee in the commissary, but quickly stepped back into the barn's darkness when he saw who was riding past him.

Ed Trumball, the U.S. Marshal who threatened to lynch him in nearby Citizen Potawatomi Reservation, had just arrived and appeared to be heading to the commandant's office.

Bat walked backwards to Buck's and Lucy's stall while trying to keep his sight on the marshal at the same time. He knew that Buck was tired from several days of scouting so he wisely saddled Lucy. Grabbing Buck by his halter, he fastened a lead rope to it and hastily rode north, this time on the flea-bit gray with Buck trailing.

******

Colonel McComber looked up from his desk when his aide, Sergeant Rumpel, opened his office door, saluted, and said, "Sir! A U. S. Marshal Ed Trumball is here. He said he needs to see you."

"Ed Trumball? Certainly! Escort him in."

As the U.S, Marshal entered the colonel's office with an air of authority, Colonel McComber stood up and greeted his old friend from the Civil War days. "Ed, good to see you! Please, sit down. You can hang your coat on the stand by the door."

Colonel McComber went back to his seat behind his oak desk and opened up his cigar box. Gesturing to Ed he asked, "Want a smoke?"

"Sounds good. Thank you."

Ed reached into the box and pulled out a cigar. After smelling the aromatic roll of tobacco leaves and biting off a tip, he placed the cigar between his lips. Striking a match on the side of his right thigh and holding the flame up to the cigar, he began puffing. After a few moments, he leaned back in his chair and slowly blew a smoke ring into the air.

The colonel sensing that his guest was comfortable and ready to talk business asked, "What brings you to Fort Reno?"

Ed slowly blew another puff of smoke into the air and responded in a calculating fashion, "Is a half-breed Potawatomi – calls himself Bat – doin' some scoutin' for you?"

"You mean John Bergeron? I do remember he referred to himself as Bat when he came in to ask about scouting. That was about seven months ago as I recall. Why do you ask?"

Ed, blowing another stream of smoke off to the side while looking directly at Colonel McComber, said, "Some of your men were down on the Choctaw Reservation a couple of weeks ago. I heard one of the scouts talk about Bat, saying that he didn't want to scout in Choctaw country. The only Bat I know is the one I run off the Citizen Potawatomi Reservation last summer. I suspected him of stealin' horses, but some of my posse didn't think so. The two men that were with him, I hung. `Cause I didn't know for sure `bout Bat, I told him to get out of the area for seven years. Your fort is too close – if it's the same Bat. I want to talk to him!"

"Sergeant Rumpel! Come in here!"

"Yes, Sir!" said the sergeant as he opened the door, stepped inside the colonel's office, and saluted."

"Find John Bergeron and bring him here," ordered Colonel McComber. "He's one of the scouts. I saw him ride in about fifteen minutes ago."

"Yes, Sir!"

Turning to Ed, the colonel asked, "Do you want a drink while we wait? I've got some brandy."

"No thanks," replied Ed. He drew in a long drag, held the smoke in his mouth for a long time, and finally blew out a steady stream of smoke. Based on having served with Ed during the Civil War, Colonel McComber knew that Ed was dealing with a serious situation.

After several minutes of waiting, there was a knock on the office door.

"Come in!" barked Colonel McComber.

The door opened. Saluting, Sergeant Rumpel said, "Sir, John Bergeron is not in the fort! Private Henderson said he saw him riding north. He had both of his horses with him and was going fast."

"Damn! It's gotta be him! He must've seen me ride in." Snuffing out his cigar and jumping up, Ed said, "Excuse me, Colonel. I'm goin' after him." He then grabbed his coat and hat as he hurried out of the commandant's office. Untying his horse, Ed jumped into his saddle, spurred his horse, and turned north after leaving the fort.

7 – Chickasaw Hosts

The marshal was an experienced tracker. Following Bat's trail was easy because there were two, fresh sets of horse tracks. The nature of the hoof prints showed that the rider was moving fast. The tracks led to the North Canadian River but soon intermingled with hundreds of cloven hoof prints left by a herd of cattle that recently had been driven across the river.

A mile north of the crossing, Bat, concerned that Marshal Trumball might have learned that he was riding north, concealed himself in a sand cherry thicket and obliterated the tracks of his horses where he had deviated from the Chisholm Trail. When the marshal rode by, Bat quietly said to himself, "Just as thought." Ever so slowly, Trumball zig-zagged back and forth across the Trail and vainly studied the ground trying to pick up Bat's trail.

Thirty minutes passed before the marshal was out of sight. As soon as Bat felt it was safe, he swiftly rode back to the Chisholm Trail and galloped south. After re-crossing the North Canadian River, he purposefully took a wide arc around Fort Reno to avoid being seen by anyone from there.

One hour later, Bat veered back to the Chisholm Trail where it crossed the South Canadian River. Speaking to Lucy, his flea-bit mare, as if she understood, Bat muttered, "We need to stop and camp, but we'd better take Buck and go a ways upstream from here. We don't want Trumball to find us. He might come this way on his way home."

Early the next morning, Bat munched on the few hard tack biscuits that he found in his saddle bags. After breaking camp, Bat searched for a safe spot where he could ford the river. Across the river was the Chickasaw Reservation, a safe area where he could ride south. He thought, "*I need to put many miles between myself and the marshal."* Bat muttered to Buck, his mount for the day, "All we gotta do is find a well-used cattle trail and follow it south into Texas. We'll figure out how to get from there to where some of my people and their Kickapoo friends settled in Mexico. First, we gotta get to Texas. I know some of my people set up camp along Dove Creek as they moved south. It can't be too far from where they went in Mexico."

The South Canadian River was notorious for its pockets of quicksand. Even the main crossing could be treacherous. Drovers who stopped at Fort Reno sometimes talked about losing cattle in the river's quicksand even though they were on the well-established Chisholm Trail.

Spurring Buck gently in the flanks, Bat pulled at the lead rope attached to Lucy and entered the reddish waters of the South Canadian River. The spot where Bat chose to ford the river had low banks on either side. *"This is easy,"* thought Bat as he approached the river's far bank. Suddenly, he heard Lucy's loud, shrill whinny. A tug on the lead rope almost dragged Bat off Buck. He looked back and saw that Lucy was in trouble.

Lucy had jumped sideways when she misconstrued a water-logged stick for a water moccasin. Her survival instincts would have been justified in the summer, but it was now winter and no snakes were out. Because Lucy had shied to the side, she had landed and was now bogged down and sinking in the dreaded quicksand. Bat had not perceived the danger.

Benjamin Arkeketa, a ten-year old Chickasaw boy, stood on an elevated, nearby bank under a leafless cottonwood tree and watched in horror at the desperate struggle that was unfolding in the river. Bat managed to get onto the river's edge and climb off Buck, but he still held tightly to Lucy's lead rope. He pulled but could not dislodge Lucy. She was sinking deeper.

Quickly, Benjamin turned and ran to get help. "Father!" he yelled as he approached his cabin. Flinging open the door, he managed to say between his gasping breaths, "A man got his horse stuck! COME!"

His father, who was seriously ill with a fever and chills, rose from his bed and struggled to find his axe. Although afflicted with malaria and a bronchial infection, he followed his son a quarter of a mile to the river.

When Benjamin got to the bluff where he had seen Bat's dilemma, he shouted, "Help's coming!" in his Chickasaw tongue. Bat didn't understand Chickasaw but figured out what the boy meant as Benjamin scooted down the bank to where Bat was standing.

Fortunately, the quicksand where Lucy had landed was not deep; and she had not struggled. Nevertheless, Lucy was stuck.

Soon, Benjamin's father arrived. Without speaking, he immediately began chopping down willow saplings and thrusting them under Lucy's belly and in front of her forelegs. After a substantial mat had been built under and in front of the horse, he and Bat began pulling firmly on the horse's lead rope.

"Help us!" shouted Bat to Lucy.

After a few moments of tugging by the two men, Lucy began lifting her forelegs. The flea-bit gray struggled but managed to climb onto the willow platform. Free from the quicksand's suction, she clamored onto the safety of the river bank.

Although the season's cold could be felt, Benjamin took off his coat and began wiping the wet sand off Lucy.

Bat looked at Benjamin's father and started to thank him, but stopped when he saw the condition of the man who now was sitting on a gray tree trunk that stuck out from a sandbar. The Chickasaw man was exhausted from cutting the willows and helping Bat pull Lucy free. He was bent over, leaning on the handle of his axe and coughing violently. It was at that moment when Bat realized that the man was not wearing a coat.

Before Bat could introduce himself and offer his gratitude, the man raised his head and said searchingly, "The river is very dangerous! I lost my wife in the quicksand last summer."

"I'm very sorry," replied Bat as he walked over to where the man was resting and put his hand on the man's shoulder. "My wife died too – late last spring – child birth." There was no reply from the one who had helped save Bat's horse.

Bat took off his coat, put it on the shoulders of the sick Chickasaw man, and sat down next to him. His own mind drifted to thoughts of his own grief and the tragic events that followed, "*Mary – where did the flood take your body? – That terrible lynching. – Boys, what's happenin' to you?*"

Several moments of silence followed as the two men watched Benjamin finish cleaning the sand off Lucy.

"Thanks," Bat finally said to the man who was sitting next to him.

"You are welcome. Benjamin, over there, came and got me. He was out looking for firewood when he saw you."

"Benjamin – is he your son?"

"Yes."

"What's your name?"

"Arkeketa."

"Arkeketa?"

"Yes, Arkeketa. I was given another name – Caleb – like in the Bible, but I usually just go by Arkeketa.

"I'm John Baptiste Bergeron but go by Bat. Can I help you back to where you live? You need to get out of this cold."

Arkeketa nodded.

Bat helped Arkeketa stand up. As he did, Arkeketa started to hand back his coat. Bat declined his coat by holding up his hands and saying, "You keep it until we get inside."

"Want some coffee when we get to the cabin? Don't have much else to offer."

"Coffee will do. Thanks."

******

As soon as the trio got back to Arkeketa's small cabin, Bat noticed that it was cold. Benjamin's father didn't waste any time climbing back onto his straw mattress and covering up with a tattered quilt. The bed itself was nothing more than a woven web of thin, willow branches.

"Benjamin, go get some firewood so we can heat up the stove. Our guest needs to have a cup of hot coffee," Arkeketa weakly said.

Benjamin promptly left. He returned ten minutes later with an armload of dry wood and started a fire in the stove. Soon, the cabin began to feel comfortably warm.

Bat, who had been invited to sit at a crude, wooden table while Benjamin tended the fire and obediently made the coffee, turned to Arkeketa and asked, "How did you get the name Caleb?"

"It came from a Methodist missionary and his wife who raised me after my parents died."

"I take it that you're Methodist."

"Yes. How about you?"

"I'm Catholic – my wife was Baptist. We even got married by a Baptist preacher when we were up in Kansas. Say, how come your English is so good?"

"My parents – the Methodist preacher and his wife – sent me away each year to the Choctaw Indian Academy in Kentucky. It's strange – we were forced to come here but sent back to school after we got here – anyway, that's where I learned English. Benjamin there knows English, but often speaks Chickasaw when he gets excited. How about you?"

"We spoke French, Potawatomi, and English at home."

"All three?"

"Yes. My father is French from Canada. My mother was Potawatomi."

"Your mother, is she dead?"

"Yes, her heart was weak."

"Sorry. "

After a pause, Bat, swirling his coffee, went on and explained more about his language background. "My father insisted we learn English – he even went by Francis, not François – but I still picked up French from him. My mother was Potawatomi, and we spoke it when some of our Potawatomi friends came to visit, We lived in Louisville, Kansas, but I attended St. Mary's mission school east of Louisville – once was a choir boy at St. Mary's – learned most of my English at the mission."

When Bat said Saint Mary's, he immediately thought of his wife and said, "My wife, Mary, died – like I said – late last spring. She was gonna have twins. They died too."

Arkeketa asked in between bouts of coughing, "Do you have any children? You are traveling alone."

"Back in Kansas, me and Mary had three children. Our first one, Joseph, died shortly before Frank – named Frank after my father – was born in 1871. About one year later, Mary had another boy, William. He was just an infant when we moved to the Indian Territory – the Citizen Potawatomi Reservation northeast of here."

"How come your sons are not with you?" inquired Areketa.

Bat appeared to go into a trance. He stared into his coffee and seemed as if he wasn't going to answer Arkeketa's question. After a few moments, Bat shifted in his chair and looked up. He was looking in Benjamin's direction, but the look on his face told Areketa that Bat was not talking to Benjamin. In the quietness of the cabin, Bat gave an account of what happened and why and where he had left his two, young sons.

Silence followed.   Arkeketa and Benjamin felt awkward. Arkeketa didn't know what to stay.

Benjamin, as if to break the uncomfortable feeling that seemed to permeate the cabin, spoke to his father, "I'm going to check the chickens. I hope we got some eggs today."

The absence of Benjamin gave Arkeketa, who had sensed despair in Bat's voice, the opportunity to speak freely to his guest. After his siege of coughing stopped, Arkeketa asked Bat, "Would you like to stay here for awhile? I have been sick for several months, and Benjamin needs some help. Your horses can be put in the corral that we passed coming up from the river. We got some oats and hay for them. We had to sell our horse so there's plenty of food for yours."

Bat barely moved his head up and down. His movement was an indication to Arkeketa that Bat was agreeable to staying.

8 – *Mi Amigo*

Fall foliage was beginning to appear. The beauty of the swaying grasses symbolized the peacefulness that Bat felt in the company of his Chickasaw hosts during the preceding seasons. In late summer after Arkeketa regained his health, Bat saddled up Buck and loaded his saddle bags with food and the other provisions that he would need to continue south on his journey.

Finding Arkeketa and Benjamin harvesting sweet potatoes in their small garden, Bat said with a catch in his voice, "Arkeketa, you and Benjamin have been very kind to me, but it's time for me to go to Mexico and find my friends down there." Bat was on Buck and trailing him was Lucy. "Benjamin, thanks to you, Lucy is alive. I don't have much, but as a way of saying thanks to you and your father, Lucy is now yours." As he handed Lucy's lead rope to Benjamin, he said, "I know you'll take good care of her." With those few words, Bat reined Buck around and headed south.

As Bat trotted along on Buck, he re-called what Joseph LaFromboise told him when they met on the West Shawnee Trail the previous summer, *"If I was by myself, I'd take everything I need with me on one horse."* His thoughts then turned to his sons, *"I wonder how they're doin'?"*

******

Just as he was told by Arkeketa, Bat reached the well-used cattle trail that fed into the Chisholm Trail by riding straight south. He then turned and rode southwest.

"Buck, I wonder how long it will take us to get to Texas?"

Bat decided to camp on the south bank of the Red River after a hard, twenty mile ride on the fifth day after getting back on the cattle trail. He would be in Texas, far from the reach of Ed Trumball, the U. S. Marshal who threatened to hang him if he did not leave the area of the Citizen Potawatomi Reservation for seven years. However, he was not certain where to go to find his friends in Mexico. All he knew is that they lived not too far southwest of a place he had heard of – Dove Creek.

"Glad there has been no rain the last two days," thought Bat as he started setting up his camp. *"With the dry grass and twigs around here, I won't have any trouble gettin' a cookin' fire started."*

Buck, who was tired and thirsty from the long trip, began prancing and pulling back from the young cotton wood tree where Bat had tied the horse's reins.

"Don't get excited, Buck. After I get done, I'll take you to the river where you can drink."

It took Bat only a few minutes to organize his camp. After unsaddling Buck, Bat said, "Now it's your turn." Buck sensed where he was going when Bat started walking him to the river. When he got to the river's edge, he pushed Bat aside with his muzzle and lowered his head for a long drink. The push caused Bat to stumble sideways, but he merely snickered.

"Hola, mi amigo!" came a deep rumbling voice.

Bat sought to regain his balance when the voice startled him and looked up to see a slimly built man entering the river from the Indian Territory side. Bat did not understand what the stranger said. He thought it was a greeting but wasn't sure.

While scrambling to regain his balance, Bat reached around Buck's neck for his saddle rifle. It wasn't there. Panic set in when he remembered that he had placed it and his pistol next to his saddle some fifteen feet away from where he and Buck were standing. Both weapons were too far from him to be of any use.

"Please my friend," said the man as he held up his free hand and continued fording the river. "I mean no harm.

I saw you from the hill behind me and saw you setting up camp. May I share your fire? I often camp at this spot when I return. I'm a drover and am returning home after herding a bunch of steers up to Kansas."

Bat relaxed when he heard the man say Kansas.

"*Buena tardes*," said the man as he dismounted from his horse and landed practically directly in front of Bat. The drover smiled, revealing a silver tooth, but then he realized that Bat wasn't Mexican and switched from Spanish to English

"I thought you were Mexican and would understand Spanish. Your skin is brown – like mine," said the stranger as he held his hand next to Bat's. "What are you?"

"Potawatomi and French."

"Potawatomi? Do you know any of the Potawatomi in Mexico?"

Bat was astounded when he heard the stranger's question. Temporarily, he was speechless but managed to say, "Yes – I want to find them!"

The drover threw his head back and laughed. As he laughed, the setting sun reflected off his silver tooth. "You want to find them?" he asked. "You'll be glad that I came along. I once had a Potawatomi wife! As a young girl, she was with a small group of Potawatomi who went to Mexico with a bunch of Kickapoo." He took his hat off and slightly bowed as if to say, "I'm at your service." When he straightened up, he flashed a big smile and said, "You're looking at your guide. I'm going home!"

"By the way, I'm Ricardo – Ricardo Pacheco. You?"

"Bat – Bat Bergeron."

"*Ricardo said he <u>once</u> had a Potawatomi wife. What did he mean?*" Bat thought.

9 – Past Memory

Bat was at the mercy of Ricardo Pacheco. Ricardo knew where he was going. Bat didn't. Ricardo had money from driving a herd of steers to Abilene, Kansas. Bat had very little. He had saved some of his Fort Reno scouting money, but spent most of it buying food for Arkeketa and Benjamin during the ten months he lived with them.

******

The next morning as the sun, a bright red fire ball, was breaking over grassy plains of the eastern horizon, the distinctively loud alarm calls from a flock of magpies stirred Bat and Ricardo. The black and white birds were mobbing a rattle snake that had slithered onto a flat rock to bask in the warmth of the rising sun. A road runner, alerted by the ruckus, had learned that such sounds meant only one thing – food. It raced in and instinctively began pecking at the snake's head. Several times, the bird agilely jumped into the air and avoided the snake's deadly fang strikes. In a few moments, the road runner subdued the snake, picked it up, and raced off with the snake's carcass dangling from its beak.

Ricardo rubbing his eyes said to Bat, "Time to wake up my friend, we have about two months of riding ahead of us, and the temperature can be hot!"

Bat and Ricardo only had one horse each. The two men realistically knew they were dependent on their horses for transportation and life in the blazing, hot Texas sun. They did not want to wear them out for the nearly five hundred-mile trip from the Red River of the South to northern Mexico where the Kickapoo and Potawatomi lived. Consequently, the men were glad if they covered only about fifteen or twenty miles per day. Every hour or so, they even walked and led their horses for fifteen minutes to rest them. It was a technique that Bat had learned while scouting at Fort Riley some ten years earlier.

******

"How often do you drive a herd from Texas to Abilene?" asked Bat.

Ricardo spit out a stream of chewing tobacco juice and took a drink of coffee. He looked at the cooking fire and said, "Once a year. I round up a herd in Texas; drive it up the Chisholm Trail, and then head back home.

"By the way," Ricardo said seriously, "many of the people in Texas are still mad about the Civil War. What I'm saying is that it's best not to even bring up the matter."

Bat half-heartedly said, "I understand." But he already was thinking about what he was going to do for the next six years. *"Should I work as a dover?"* he asked himself. However, the thought of passing close to Ed Trumball's marshalling territory made him cringe, and the Chisholm Trail passed through the western part of it. Still a vivid memory in his mind was the vision of the horse thieves dying from strangulation when they were lynched on short ropes.

******

The ride south through Texas was a two-man traveling school. Bat traded Potawatomi history lessons for Spanish lessons. Ricardo listened patiently to Bat, but was courteous in not telling him that he had heard his wife explain much of the Potawatomi history when they were married. On the other hand, Ricardo's Spanish lessons were relished by Bat.

For two solid weeks, he and Bat conversed only in Spanish. Occasionally, Bat had to ask Ricardo how to say a word in Spanish, but his rapidly developing fluency in the language was a pleasant surprise to the teacher.

Often on the trail drives north, some of the English-speaking drovers refused to learn any Spanish. Ricardo once nicknamed a drover, Tommy *poco*. The man thought that it was a complimentary name, not realizing that he was, in fact, being chided by Ricardo for not learning much Spanish.

As the horses plodded steadily south, Ricardo talked about his experiences working on the Chisholm Trail. "When I first started going on the Trail, the trail boss thought I was too small, so he made me a cook's helper – he made me ride on the chuck wagon – mostly I fetched water and scrubbed pans. It wasn't until two years ago that I actually became a drover."

"Once, us Mexican cowboys had to round up some buffalo. We chased 'em into special pens and loaded 'em into really strong cattle cars. We already were in Kansas then."

"Why did you get buffalo?" questioned Bat with a slight smirk on his face. "They're ornery."

"Yes, we quickly found out. It was hard to hold them, but we finally got 'em into the railroad cars. Some guy – he was all dressed up in a suit – was taking 'em to Chicago. I was told that he was gonna use the buffalo to advertise bringing beef from Kansas. I got to go along. Some short guy with a black patch over one eye and a white beard met us in Illinois. A stockyard worker told me his name was Hubbard – very distinctive because of his black patch. Speaking of Illinois – know where I mean?"

"Yes," replied Bat. "I used to live there. I even heard my mother mention Hubbard – might even be the same guy – once in awhile – gathered that they once were married – the old Indian way."

Sensing that he had touched on a sore subject, Ricardo quickly changed the conversation. "What took you to the Indian Territory? You told me once that you came down the Chisholm Trail from Kansas and settled next to the Seminoles."

"We were given citizenship and land allotments in Kansas, but a lot of people lost their land because of greedy bank people and the railroad – the same one that took you and the buffalo to Chicago. A few years ago we were told we could move to the Indian Territory. However, we had to pay for the land even though it was called the Citizen Potawatomi Reservation."

"How come you left the – Citizen Potawatomi Reservation?"

Bat was silent, and Ricardo decided not to ask him any more questions. Instead, Ricardo told Bat some more of his drover experiences. "One thing we learned was not to take the herds all the way to Kansas too early in the season."

"I gather that you probably ran into a late spring blizzard," interjected Bat.

"Not only that, but there wasn't much grazing grass for the steers if we got 'em there before the first of May."

"We had one really bad drive," said Ricardo looking over at Bat.

"Oh! What?" inquired Bat.

"Black leg – we had to shoot the whole herd. We were only seventy-five miles from Abilene – that's where we were gonna load the steers onto railroad cars."

******

"CATCH HIM AND GRAB HIM BY THE TAIL! USE THE BUTT OF YOUR PISTOL AND CLONK HIM ON THE HEAD," shouted Ricardo. "Somehow, we need to get some fresh meat." Laughing he said, "I'll hold Buck's reins for you! Run faster!"

Bat was in pursuit of an armadillo, an animal that Bat had never seen before. It had trotted across the trail that he and Ricardo were on. *This is gonna be easy,* thought Bat even though sweat covered his forehead and upper torso because of the Texas heat. The ground was strewn with rocks and rocky crevices; and the armadillo used them to elude Bat's grasp. Finally, the armadillo Bat was chasing sought shelter in a deep crevice.

"WATCH OUT FOR RATTLERS!" hollered Ricardo from the safety of his horse. He was amused by the chase.

Just then Bat felt a sharp, burning sting on his right hand. Quickly, he pulled his hand out of the crevice and saw that the back of his hand had two, slightly bloody puncture marks. By the time he jerked out his hand, it already was tingling, and he could feel his right arm getting numb.

Seeing what had happened, Ricardo jumped off his horse. He led Bat to the shade of a live oak tree and began efforts to stop the spread of the rattle snake's poison and save his friend. Quickly, he chewed up the roots of several nearby sunflowers and rubbed the paste into the puncture marks on Bat's hand. In this manner, the paste neutralized the poison's potency. The perspiration on Bat's forehead was an indication to Ricardo that not all of the poison had been caught in time. Over the next week, Bat slowly recovered and fortunately showed no extensive necrotic skin damage. Fortunately, no arteries of major veins on the back of Bat's hand had been punctured.

"What saved you," said Ricardo one day when he was nursing Bat back to health, "is that the rattler was small because the two bite marks were very close together."

"Where did you learn your treatment?" asked Bat between bouts of deliria. "We always cut the bites and suck out the poison."

"Didn't always work, did it? Some of the Indians in these parts know better ways. I learned my treatment from them. If you have the strength, come over to the fire. I managed to shoot some jackrabbits today. They're a little chewy, but at least we have meat. The horses are fine. They found patches of grass to eat and are getting water from a little spring up in the rocks. It has been nice of them to let me have some of the water."

"I had a vision that the trees were growing golden hair," said Bat.

Ricardo chuckled. "You didn't have a vision. A friend told me that what looks like hair on the trees around here is a parasite. He called it a small mistletoe or something like that. It's common. Take a look at the tree branches above you. I see the same thing. It's on all the trees."

Bat's snake bite was not the only thing that slowed down the journey of Bat and Ricardo. From time to time, they successfully sought out hired-hand work, especially to work as cowboys for the area's ranchers who needed help rounding up cattle for fall branding and castrating.

Bat and Ricardo spent a night camping by the Brazos River. Using his saddle as his pillow and staring up at the brilliant twinkling stars, Ricardo took the occasion to ask Bat about his background. "Bat, you have talked a lot about Kansas – were you born there?"

"Yes," replied Bat, "but I lived in other places too – Illinois, Iowa, – Nebraska."

"If you were born in Kansas, how did you come to live in the other places?"

"My mother married my father in Illinois," said Bat sliding his saddle blanket off Buck.

"You said some time back that you're the oldest – your mother and father must have gone to Kansas after they got married."

"First, it was just my mother. She told me that my father came to Kansas just before I was born. Then we all went to Illinois."

"Wait, first Kansas, then Illinois. How do Iowa and Nebraska fit in because you said you lived in Kansas before you moved to Indian Territory just a couple of years ago?"

"It's complicated," replied Bat unrolling his bed roll and lying down. "The government kept making us move."

"Got any children?" asked Ricardo, but his question went unanswered.

Ricardo turned and looked at Bat. He could not help notice that Bat had his gaze fixed on the night sky and appeared to be caught in the web of a past memory.

48

10 – Rider at Dove Creek

One evening while reaching for the coffee pot propped up on stones by the camp fire, Ricardo cautioned, "Bat, don't mention the word Kickapoo. We're getting close to Dove Creek and for a few years after a battle there between the Kickapoo and Potawatomi against a bunch of ignorant Texans there, the Kickapoo carried out retaliatory border raids along the Rio Grande. I know – at least used to know – the ones who went on the raiding parties. Some of the same ranchers we want to work for might have gotten raided or at least their neighbors did."

"The cattle we work with today," continued Ricardo, "probably will be the ones I help round up next spring and drive to Kansas – and I need cattle so don't say anything about the Kickapoo."

******

"Bat, see the tree-line over there. It's Dove Creek. We'll stop there for the night. I know the rancher who owns the land where we can camp. Maybe he'll have some work for us," said Ricardo.

"How do you know him?" asked Bat.

"I helped take some of his cattle to market – up the Chisholm Trail – three years ago. We drove the first herd that year and got a good price for his steers. He was real happy."

"Three years ago? That would be the same year that I left Kansas. The group that I was with didn't see a herd until we got to the North Canadian River. There was a whole lot of shootin' so me and another guy snuck up to see what was goin' on. My brother-in-law was guidin' us and thought we might be runnin' into a fight of some kind.

Grinning, Ricardo looked at Bat and said, "That was us," he replied. "For some reason, the herd didn't want to go across the North Canadian so we really started shooting and hollering to scare 'em across. Sometimes, it's done that way."

"What do you know about a battle at Dove Creek? You've mentioned it a couple of times," inquired Bat.

"Let's talk about it tonight. First, let's go see Richard Tankersley. He owns the land we'll be on and might have some work for us. He usually does. That's his place over yonder." As Ricardo said this, he spurred his horse into a fast trot. Soon, Bat caught up with him.

******

Ricardo turned around and saw Bat pushing aside branches. They were making their way through the thicket that bordered much of Dove Creek. Seeing that Bat was close behind, he said, "Up ahead not too far is a clearing where we can camp for the night."

"I hope you're right," muttered Bat. *"This stuff is worse than goin' through Cross Timbers,"* he thought.

Whap! A branch nearly knocked Bat off Buck.

Just then the thick brush gave way to a wide clearing on the east bank of Dove Creek. It was the same clearing that the Kickapoo and Potawatomi had selected for their overwintering village in the waning months of the Civil War, a conflict they wanted to escape.

Bat stopped Buck. The scenic clearing with Dove Creek's clear flowing water was a refreshing contrast to the rocky and semi-arid, hot Texas terrain that he had ridden through for several weeks. He gently kicked Buck in the flanks and rode to the stream. There, he stopped and let Buck drink. Bat patiently waited for Buck to lift his head before reining him back and turning him around.

Ricardo already had unsaddled his horse and was leading it to Dove Creek. As he passed Bat, he said, "Good place, huh? After you unsaddle your horse, look around for some wood that we can use to cook the meat that Tankersley gave us."

******

"Who wants to go first?" Ricardo asked. "You already know something about the battle that took place here. I'm interested in what you have to say – Bat?"

Bat seemed to be caught up in a hypnotic trance. Finally, he shook his head and said, "I heard about the fight from Joseph Bourassa – a couple of the Bourassa men married Potawatomi. The Potawatomi who went with the Kickapoo to Mexico were friends and relatives of ours. The connection goes back to when my mother lived on the Pickamick River in Illinois – not too far from the Kickapoo – also in Illinois. The Potawatomi from the Pickamick joined the Kickapoo near Fort Leavenworth after they were made to leave their homes in Illinois."

"Our family almost moved to Mexico too, but my father still was recoverin' from his hearin' loss. He fought against the Confederates in Westport, Missouri. After that fight, Josette, my mother, didn't want any more to do with the Civil War. He – we – would've gotten into another fight had we come."

"I thought you once said your mother's name was Watchekee," interrupted Ricardo.

"Watchekee was her Potawatomi name. Her baptized name was Josette. She was Catholic. So were most people that we knew, and they called her Josette – her baptized name," answered Bat to clear up the confusion. "The way my mother pronounced her name it sounded like Zozzette."

"Anyway, Joseph went so far as to send a letter to some Texan officials to see if he could find out if they knew whether or not any our people were killed in the fight. If so,

51

he was hoping to get their names. He didn't ever hear back. Perhaps I can find out some day."

"About one thousand Kickapoo and Potawatomi left the reservations in Kansas to stay out of the Civil War that was beginning to get close. Lots of people got scared and didn't know the war was ending. Those that came through here got permission from the Indian Agent – up in Kansas – to leave and go to Mexico. The ones that tried to camp here were led by No-kah-ta – he's Kickapoo. He and most of the others with him once lived north of Fort Leavenworth. My mother once lived there too. In fact, that's where I was born."

"It wasn't until No-kah-ta's band got here that there was any trouble. First, they talked to Tankersley – the same one you know – and he told them they could set up a winter camp here – from what I see, probably this spot. The people didn't want to harm anyone."

"A bunch of Confederates and Texas militia – soldiers – if that's what you want to call them – picked up the trail of No-kah-ta's band – only about 120 people."

"My people set up their wigwams and were set up to have a peaceful camp. A few days later, the soldiers arrived – then BAM!" Bat began to explain.

Waving his right arm toward the thicket through which he and Ricardo had ridden, he continued, "Three elders, two men and one woman, walked out to talk with the soldiers. They had a white flag of truce and started to show the note to the soldiers that their Indian Agent had given to them. Aski tried to shake hands of an officer soldier. Without warning, the officer shot and killed Aski. That started the fight."

"Many of the attackers were wounded or killed. My people were well-armed with Enfield rifles and were good shots. The thicket and draws to the creek gave them lots of cover. The soldiers had no idea what they were up against."

"A boy who had climbed up a cottonwood tree just before the soldiers came saw the fightin'. He said that our women even got involved in the fight by rushin' out with fryin' pans and knockin' some of the soldiers off their horses. The soldiers were routed from what I understand."

"After the fight, my people decided not to stay here for the winter. They quickly broke camp, formed a protective circle around the women, children and wounded, crossed the Rio Grande, and fled into Mexico."

"You told me that Bourassa sent a letter asking for information about the fight, but never found out anything. Do you know how many people on your side died?" queried Ricardo.

"About twelve, including a child," solemnly replied Bat. He was deep in thought, *"What if my family and me were here then?"*

"Shh," suddenly whispered Ricardo. He quietly put down his coffee mug, held up his finger to his lips as a signal for Bat to be quiet, and silently lifted his revolver out of its holster. "Quickly, move away from the fire and get in the dark – someone's coming. Get your gun ready!" he said in a hushed voice.

Instinctively, Bat armed himself.

Scurrying quietly to the safety of the dark brush and remaining still, Bat and Ricardo heard a slow but distinct clip-clop of a horse and the cursing of a man making his way through the thicket.

Bat whispered to Ricardo. "I think there's only one rider."

In a few moments, a single man emerged into the opening. Looking around and peering into the darkness in an attempt to see someone, he shouted, "I seen your fire! Mind if I join you! I'm peaceful!"

Warily, Bat and Ricardo emerged from their dark hiding place. The stranger, seeing reflective glints on gun barrels, knew that he could get shot if he wasn't careful. He slowly raised his left arm to signify his peaceful intent.

"Get you right arm up too!" commanded Bat.

"I can't. It's useless."

Ricardo had a good view of the stranger. Speaking sideways out of his mouth, he said to Bat, "I think he's telling the truth!" Squinting to get a better look at the man, he said, "Look, his gun's on his left hip." He then directed his voice to the stranger and said, "Slowly get off your horse and get out in the open so we can get a better look at you."

"Keep a look out, Bat! He's no drover – no lariat. – It wouldn't do him any good anyway if he's got only one good arm. He might have friends in the brush – waiting to shoot us! We gotta be careful!"

The stranger dismounted his horse, turned to Bat and Ricardo and quietly but nervously said, "I'm alone."

When assured that the man was being truthful, Bat and Ricardo holstered their pistols.

Bat returned to where had had been sitting while Ricardo talked to the stranger.

"I'm Ricardo, my friend over there is Bat. What's your name?"

"Marvin," replied the man with the limp, right arm.

"After you get your horse taken care of, come and join us. This time of the year, there's water in the creek, and there's plenty of grass over on that side of the clearing. You should be able to make out or hear our horses. Ours are hobbled. You might want to do the same with yours."

"Thanks," said Marvin.

Ricardo returned to the cooking fire and soon was joined by Marvin.

In silence, Bat sat staring at the fire. He seemingly was oblivious to Marvin's presence.

"We got lots of beef and potatoes cooking. We've got coffee too. Want some?"

"Yep."

The gulping and slurping sounds that Marvin made while he drank and ate starkly contrasted to the slowness of his movements.

"Where you coming from?" asked Ricardo.

"Eastern Colorado – along its border with Kansas," answered Marvin. "To save you from askin' – I'm headed to southern Louisiana."

"How did you hurt your arm?"

Ricardo's question made Marvin slightly grimace as he rubbed his right shoulder.

"Got shot," responded Marvin without looking at Ricardo.

"War injury?"

"Nope." Then, almost as if speaking to himself, Marvin began explaining the circumstance of his injury.

"Me and Steve – he was my partner – fought on the Confederate side. We didn't get a scratch during the war – were in some pretty tough fightin'. After the war, we set out lookin' fer work. Once in Indian Territory we were ridin' up the Arbuckle Wagon Road, north of the main Canadian river on the Potawatomi Reservation." Looking at Ricardo, Marvin asked, "Know where I mean?"

Ricardo gave a slight head nod to signify that he understood, but purposefully did not say anything in hopes that Marvin would keep talking. Ricardo especially avoided any reference to Bat having come from the Potawatomi Reservation. The ploy worked.

"Along the way, we spotted a fella bustin' sod. He had just turned west, away from the road. His oxen were heavin' and snortin' so much that he didn't hear us ridin' up. Steve decided to have some fun. He roped the man and begun draggin' him through a big, red mud puddle. It had rained hard the day before. Steve was draggin', and the man was hollerin' and a splashin' through the mud. All of a sudden, this old Indian woman comes out of her cabin with a rifle and started shootin'. She shot Steve clean off his horse. I turned to skedaddle, but the woman shot again and hit me in the shoulder. I didn't know if Steve was still alive so when I got to the wagon road, I stopped. I was bleedin' and hurt, but I figured if I had chance, I was gonna go back and get him.

Just as I turned around to look, the woman came back out of her cabin with a knife and scalped Steve. I seen all of it."

Bat suddenly realized who Marvin was talking about, his mother and father. In spite of what Marvin was saying, he remained stoic because his thoughts kept focusing on other personal trauma: "*Mary – babies died too – bodies washed away – nearly got lynched – abandoned my boys.*"

"How did you get you wound treated?" asked Ricardo.

"I rode south to the Choctaw Reservation and found a doctor. While I was being treated, Ed Trumball, a U. S. Marshal, happened to be around. He come by and after talkin' to me said that he would find the woman and deal with her."

"Found out later, the woman's name was Josette Bergeron," said Marvin as he swirled the coffee in his cup.

Ricardo tensed when he heard Marvin say "Bergeron."

Marvin kept on talking. "Accordin' to what I heard, the marshal was mad 'cause he rode all the way to where this Josette lived and found out that he couldn't even talk to her. She was dead."

"After I got healed, I rode up to Colorado. I tried gold mining but couldn't do the work so I joined the Kanorado Outlaws. We once robbed a man who had a French accent. He looked just like the fella that Steve drug through the mud 'fore he was shot," said Marvin. He shook his head. "Naw! It couldn't have been him!"

Bat started seriously listening at this point and heard what Marvin said about his mother and how the marshal reacted when he learned that she had died before he dealt with her. "*I think I now know what the marshal meant when he said 'How come you Bergerons are always causing me problems?'*"

The change in how his family was now perceived deepened Bat's despondent mood. "*Back in Kansas, our family was respected. I heard my father was even once an election judge. Now we're thought of as no gooders causing problems.*" Bat then got up and strolled over to the bank of Dove Creek. He sat down and took off his hat. Ricardo glanced over and saw the darkened silhouette of Bat who by now had put his head into his hands. Ricardo began to realize how deeply Marvin's talking had affected Bat.

Bat now was thinking about how to kill Marvin. However, he decided not to go through with his thoughts. "*I nearly got lynched along with the horse thieves. Don't want to try explainin' myself to another marshal. I might come out on the losin' end again!*"

Ricardo meanwhile had other ideas. "*I'll wait until morning to kill Marvin so I can hide his body better. It's too dark now to find a good place.*" Resting his head on his saddle and pulling up his blanket, he thought, "*Time to get some sleep now.*"

******

"Caw! Caw!" The racket made by a family of crows that had roosted in the nearby woods awakened Ricardo just after the first light of the day started creeping over the eastern horizon. He stretched and reached for his pistol. Turning over to face Marvin, he gasped. The place where Marvin had slept was empty. He looked around to see if he could see any sign of Marvin, whom he had come to detest. Everything was gone – saddle, bridle, horse.

Throwing back his blanket, he shook Bat and said, "Get up! Marvin snuck out sometime during the night!"

"So?" replied a sleepy-eyed Bat. In a few moments, he realized that Marvin actually was gone. "Good!" he said under his breath.

Ricardo acted as if he had not heard Bat's utterance. After all, he had not told Bat of what he planned to do. All he could do was mutter to himself, "Marvin must have known what was gonna happen. Guess he figured that he talked too much last night."

******

As the cooking fire crackled, Ricardo asked Bat, "Know anything about what Marvin was saying last night?"

"Yep," quietly answered Bat as he slurped his coffee.

"What?"

Bat stood up and emptied his coffee into the fire. "My folks."

"How come you didn't get mad."

"I did, but I had lots of things on my mind – especially my sons. I had to leave them."

Bat's eyes became misty.

Ricardo, at that point, realized a little of what Bat had been keeping to himself.

Bat and Ricardo spent the next three days at Dove Creek. The interlude gave them time to bathe in the creek and provide their horses a deserved rest.

On the morning of the fourth day, Ricardo shouted, "BAT! Time to break camp and head for Eagle Pass! SADDLE UP!"

Bat already was leading Buck in from the meadow when Ricardo hollered. After getting to the clearing where he and Ricardo had camped, he laid the saddle blanket carefully over his horse's back and threw on the saddle. Buck had developed the habit of deeply inhaling and holding his breath when ever Bat saddled him. It made cinching him difficult. Once, shortly after Buck was broken, the saddle tipped sideways and unceremoniously dumped Bat on the ground. Ever since, Bat routinely gave Buck a hard knee thrust in the rib cage as he cinched the saddle. Bat's technique caused Buck to release his held breath. With his saddle securely cinched, Bat reached for his saddle bags.

Before tying the saddle bags behind the saddle, Bat opened them and looked inside them to make certain that he had everything for the ride to Eagle Pass. As he was rummaging through the left bag, he saw it. Instantly, he realized what it was. Carefully, Bat took out a brown clay marble.

"What is it?" curiously asked Ricardo. He was waiting impatiently for Bat to get on Buck so they could leave camp. Instead, Bat was standing next to Buck staring at an object in his hand.

"It's a marble my father made for me when I was a boy. He wanted me to have something to play with. It was my birthday present when I turned nine. We were living in Louisville, Kansas at the time."

"So?"

"I want my boys to have it – some day they will – I hope."

Ricardo showed no interest in the marble. He already was talking about trail business: "When we get to Rocksprings – a little place not far north of Eagle Pass – I need to stop and settle up with some ranchers. I got my last herd there. The ranchers want to be paid in gold. They don't want any Yankee money – as they call it – still fighting your Civil War I guess.

11 – Orphanage

Kate cried "Any word about Bat?" as her husband, Joe, came stumbling into the cabin's kitchen in what had become routine – a drunken stupor. Kate had learned she could tell when he was drunk if she heard him singing at the top of his voice as his buggy came down the wagon road leading up to their cabin.

"He's been gone for nearly three years – just vanished!" continued Kate. "About all we know is that the Indian Agent from up in Shawneetown brought us Frank and Will to take care of. Remember seeing the note his wife found in Frank's shirt when she was gettin' ready to give the boys a bath?"

Joe had returned from Wanette, a small village that formed after he and Kate and a handful of other Potawatomi moved from Kansas to the new reservation in 1872. He wasn't in any mood to discuss the whereabouts of Bat.

"Naw!" he slurred. "*Quay* (woman), bring me some coffee!"

Kate knew there was going to be trouble whenever Joe called her *Quay,* but she dutifully picked up the coffee pot off the blackened stove and carried it over to where Joe was sitting. He was slumped forward with his head resting on the rough-hewn, kitchen table. Kate did not know what to expect, but she was growing weary of Joe's explosions and verbal abuse.

Her older children were out cutting hay, but three children were with her in the kitchen, Frank and Will, Bat's sons, and her one-year old baby, Louie. Joe was the baby's father. She knew from experience that the three children had to be gotten out of the room for their own safety. Racing through her mind was the time that Joe had violently shaken Louie in a raging but vain attempt to muffle the baby's cries.

Fearing for their safety, Kate quietly ordered, "Frank and Will, take little Louie with you and go outside."

"The sun is really hot today!" whined Frank.

"Just do as I say! Now hurry!"

"Come on, Will. I'll get Louie," said Frank somewhat disgustedly. Finally, he picked up Louie and headed out the cabin doorway.

Will rushed outside to play with the 'mama' cat whose five kittens were tumbling on the ground beside her.

"When did she bring her kittens out of the corn crib?" asked Frank. Before Will could answer, the attention of both boys turned to the sounds of loud voices and scuffling coming from the cabin.

When Kate had started pouring Joe a cup of coffee, he grabbed her and tried to kiss her. Kate could smell his alcoholic breath and felt the stubble of his three-day growth. She started to push him away. Reacting to Kate's resistance, Joe struck her across the face and pushed her to the floor. Quickly, she got to her feet and armed herself with a butcher knife. Seeing that he was facing a determined woman, Joe teetered and said, "You bitch!"

"OUT!" Kate hollered. "I'M THROUGH WITH YOU!"

Frank and Will saw Joe stagger from the cabin and struggle to get on a nearby horse and ride away. At the same time, they heard sobbing coming from the cabin.

Frank peeked through the doorway and saw Kate hunched and sitting at the table. She was crying, and the butcher knife was lying on the floor beside her. Although she was sobbing, Frank understood her say, "What'm I gonna do with all the children?"

******

Whack! Kate's hatchet lopped off the head of another unfortunate chicken. Frank and Will delighted in chasing down the headless creature. After they chased it down, they plunged it into a kettle of boiling water to loosen up the feathers so they could be easily plucked. Two of Kate's children, Leander and Tom, were assigned to pull the chickens out of the boiling water, pluck them, and eviscerate them.

Little Joe held another chicken that was to lose its cranium and thereby contribute to the canned supply of the family's protein. Benjamin chased and caught others that fluttered around the chicken coup.

It was three months after Joe had left, and Kate was struggling to mother her children and exhaustedly worked to bring in the crops and care for the livestock. *"Somehow, I've got to preserve and can enough food to see us through the winter,"* she worriedly thought.

It was mid-afternoon when she finished her work with the chickens and wiped the perspiration off her forehead that she heard the incessant honking of her gaggle of geese. The commotion sent her dog into howling and barking.

Kate knew that a visitor was coming and walked through her cabin's 'dog trot' to see who.

She smiled when she saw Father Rote riding his horse down the lane toward the cabin. After all, he used her cabin to celebrate the first Mass held on the Reservation.

"Good afternoon, Father," said Kate as she used the apron on her skirt to wipe off chicken blood. While standing in the doorway leading into the kitchen, she gestured and added, "Please come in and sit down."

"Thank you," Father Rote graciously replied.

Kate signified for Father Rote to take a seat by the kitchen table.

"Can I get you somethin' to drink? Coffee? Somethin' cool?"

"If you got something cool, I'll take it," answered Father Rote as he laid his black, priestly hat on the table.

"Little Joe go to the well and pull up some grape juice for Father," directed Kate.

While waiting for Little Joe to return, Kate twisted around to see the priest and asked, "What brings you this way?"

Father Rote cleared his throat before drinking the cool juice that Little Joe had fetched. The mannerism told Kate that the Father had something important to discuss.

"Is it true that you and Joe are no longer married?" started Father Rote.

Realizing the seriousness of the priest's visit, Kate turned to the children and said, "Little Joe, take all the children outside. Make sure that no one gets hurt – stay away from the kettle of hot water and the hatchet." She turned and spoke directly to Father Rote. "Yes, Joe left. He got to be mean to me so I told him to leave and never come back."

Father Rote took a sip of his grape juice and without looking at Kate said, "You know that the Church does not condone your action."

"Yes, I know."

"In part, that's why I'm here. The other reason is the children."

"The children?" asked Kate as she furrowed her brow.

"Yes, the children. Taking care of such a large family must be hard. I'm especially thinking of the added responsibility of raising Bat's sons by yourself."

"You talkin' 'bout Frank and Will?"

"Yes."

"What 'bout them?"

"It doesn't seem that Bat is ever going to come back. Some people think that he is dead."

Kate's eyes welled up when Father Rote mentioned that her brother might be dead. She wiped her tears with her apron, the same apron that she wore when cutting the heads off her chickens. It was covered with dried spatters of chicken blood. Her attempt to clear her eyes left brownish-red streaks across her upper cheeks.

Father Rote clasped Kate's hands in his, looked at her blood-streaked face, and continued, "We're starting a boarding school and orphanage at Sacred Heart. The Church can help you out if you let Frank and Will stay at the orphanage."

Kate thought, *"Break up the family?"* She started to whimper and protest what Father Rote had offered.

"Think about it," said Father Rote. He finished drinking the last of his grape juice, picked up his hat, and said, "Excuse me now. I need to get back to Sacred Heart while there still is some light." Quietly, Father Rote slipped out the door and got back on his horse.

Kate had followed Father Rote out of the cabin, still deep in thought about what the Father had said about Frank and Will going to the new orphanage.

Father Rote mounted his horse, looked down at Kate, and repeated his last statement, "Think about it. Good day." He then reined his horse around and headed east toward Sacred Heart.

******

Two days later, Kate said, "Frank and Will, get in the buggy."

Frank and Will had lost their mother during childbirth and their father when he abandoned them. For a short period they had a stable life albeit in a dysfunctional family. They did not realize it, but they were starting the next phase of their life's journey, a phase of which Bat would have no involvement. After all, he had been exiled from the Citizen Potawatomi Reservation by U. S. Marshal Ed Trumball.

12 – Border Towns

Ricardo looked over at Bat and asked, "Ready for a new culture?"

"What'cha mean?" replied Bat.

"I know you know the Potawatomi culture and language as well as the English and French languages, but your Spanish soon will be needed," said Ricardo. "Look over there. See the tree line? It's along the Rio Grande – the border between the U.S.A. and Mexico. The little town you see ahead of us is Eagle Pass. It's the last English-speaking settlement in Texas. We're gonna ride through town and cross over a bridge. When we do, we'll be in Piedras Negras and in Mexico – home as far as I'm concerned. We'll spend a couple of days resting up there."

Bat detected excitement in Ricardo's voice. Still he wasn't quite sure about what Ricardo meant by being ready for a new culture so he asked, "What will being in Piedras Negras – Mexico – gonna mean to me?"

Ricardo threw his head back and laughed, "You will see my friend. By the way, when we go through Eagle Pass, watch out for a man with two, pearl-handled pistols. He probably will be looking straight ahead and won't say anything. If he does, just tip your hat and ride on by. Give him lots of room."

"How's that?" asked Bat.

"I'll explain later." With his reply, Ricardo looked at Bat, loosened the reins on his own horse, and spurred it into a run. Bat kicked Buck and raced after him. When Bat caught up to Ricardo, they were close to Eagle Pass. Upon reaching the town, they slowed their horses down to a walk.

The main street through Eagle Pass was fairly crowded. The people in the street either were riding in buggies, on wagons, or on single horses. Some of them were walking. Bat sniffed the air and smelled an odor that was a mixture of the smoke coming from charcoal ovens and the distinctive aroma of horse dung. The wagons leaving town were filled with sacks of flour, salt, sugar, and corn plus some had rolls of wire and assorted tack. One even had an upright piano.

Bat observed and thought, *"The loaded wagons I'm seein' must be headed for ranches near here."*

Ricardo had a much different thought. *"Not too many years ago, this place wasn't but a trading post."*

Some of the single riders were cowboys judging by their chaps, hats, boots, and spurs. Also they had well-pummeled saddles, loosely tied to which were lariats. Others were cavalry soldiers on leave from nearby Fort Duncan, an outpost of Fort Clark that had the dubious honor of flying the last Confederate flag before it was taken down and thrown into the Rio Grande.

Bat noticed that Ricardo's body stiffened and a contemptuous scowl spread over his face whenever a soldier rode by.

Suddenly, the street was empty except for three riders, two were headed south and one was riding north. Bat and Ricardo merely were riding in tandem through town to the bridge that spanned the Rio Grande.

Ricardo kept his sight on the single rider. Without hesitating when he saw reflections coming off the rider's pistol handles and their white pearl adornments, he whispered, "Bat – ride slowly and don't make any sudden moves. Keep your hands away from your waist and remember what I told you. Tip your hat only if he says anything, but don't say anything to him. It's him – Fisher!"

Bat heeded Ricardo's instructions as they approached the lone rider and heard Ricardo breathe a sigh of relief after they got several yards down the street past Fisher.

Stores along the way earlier had opened their doors to capture breezes and thereby counter the afternoon heat.

Now, the doorways were clogged with people gawking at the riders who were riding in opposite directions.

"Look at the people in the doorways. It's as if they're expectin' something to happen. What's with that fella who just rode by us?" asked Bat.

"Like I said, I'll tell you later. We'll be in Piedras Negras as soon as we cross the Rio Grande. I'll tell you there."

13 – *Candelabras*

Antonio Gutierrez was standing behind his bar of the Alba Aqua Cantina in Piedras Negras, when Ricardo strolled in with his jingling spurs and yelled in his deep rumbling voice, "HELLO! I'M BACK!"

"I see or should I say I hear?" said Antonio as he smiled broadly. Bat clearly saw that Antonio also flashed a silver tooth above his well-groomed mustache. Its reflection matched the twinkle in Antonio's eyes. Without hesitating, Antonio stepped around the end of the bar and warmly embraced Ricardo. The two men stood looking at each other and slapping each other on the back. Bat thought, *"They must be old friends."*

"VERONICA!" shouted Antonio as he turned his head around to direct his voice to the back of the cantina. "Come see who's back from pushing longhorns up to Kansas!"

Bat looked in the same direction and saw strings of beads and a short hallway beyond the beads. Soon, the beads made a rustling sound and a rather plump, middle-aged woman emerged. It was Veronica, Antonio's wife, coming from the living quarters.

As soon as Veronica saw Ricardo, she covered her mouth with her hands and in a shout of joy she broke into hysteria of sobs and laughs. Extending her arms, she rushed toward Ricardo and hugged and kissed him several times."Ricardo, every time you come back – how long have you been gone this time – eight months?"

"I've never seen so much emotion," thought Bat. His mind suddenly was flooded with past memories: *"Mary's agonizin' cries in childbirth – the loss of Mary – even her*

body – the trustin' innocence on the faces of my sons when I left them on the porch of the Indian Agent."

Bat still was lost in thought when Antonio asked, "Ricardo! Who's your friend?" Bat quickly came back into the conversation when he heard Antonio's question.

"Oh! Antonio, this is Bat – Bat Bergeron. Bat, this is my sister, Veronica – and her husband, Antonio. He then put his arms around his sister and Antonio and pulled them to his sides.

Antonio broke away and said, "Ricardo, let me get you something to drink. You look thirsty. Whadda you want – a glass of *cerveza* (beer)? How about you, Bat?"

"Give him some tequila. It's the first time Bat's come to Mexico!" Ricardo said with a grin.

Bat started to protest, "I haven't had a drink since just before I got married. My wife was Baptist."

"Never mind Bat. Antonio, give my friend some tequila." "Watch out for the agave worm!" laughed Ricardo as he slapped Bat on the back and slid a bottle of tequila in front of him.

******

A buzzing headache greeted Bat the next morning. Finally, he stretched and shook his head trying to clear it. Looking up from his bed and through a window, he saw Veronica cooking on a charcoal stove in the adjoining court yard. He staggered to the door leading to the outside kitchen and started admiring its setting. It had a bed of beavertail cacti under a Palo Verde tree. A few *Yucca* plants and a single *Agave*, Spanish bayonet or century plant, completed the landscaping.

Veronica sensed Bat's presence and started jabbering without even glancing at him, "Want some coffee? It's made from the roasted seeds of okra, but tastes like coffee. We learned to use okra seeds after coffee was hard to get during your fighting – your Civil War. I'll have some burritos ready soon. Come out and enjoy the sun. We have lots of it here."

After breakfast, Bat left the cantina and saw that it faced the town's plaza. A sense of relief overcame him as he stood in the morning sun. He thought, "*I'm completely out of Trumball's jurisdiction.*"

In a relaxed fashion, Bat wandered about Piedras Negras after first checking on Buck. He soon noticed a seemingly care-free attitude of the people whom he met. Yet, everyone was working hard, especially those who were placing bags of candles and hanging strings of dry, red peppers in rows around the plaza.

Antonio was sitting and talking to three customers when Bat returned to the cantina. Just as Bat entered, Ricardo came through the cascade of beads. He saw Bat and pointed to a table that had a good view of the plaza. As the two of them sat down, Ricardo softly whistled to get Veronica's attention. "Bring us some coffee."

While they waited for Veronica to serve them, Ricardo said, "Guess you figured that this is where we'll rest up."

Before Bat could respond, Veronica came with the coffee that Ricardo ordered. She gave Ricardo a beaming smile when she put a pewter cup of the steaming brew in front of him. She was glad to have her baby brother back.

"Ricardo," Bat said, "you seemed worried when you saw a man you called 'Fisher.' Is he the man you told me to watch out for?"

"Fisher, you mean John Fisher?"

"I guess so. Was he the man you were tellin' me about?"

Ricardo put down his cup, looked at Bat and began to chuckle. "Yes. He's the man I was talking about. He fancies himself as a gunfighter – you know shoot first – ask later. He came down from north of Dallas a few years ago. Supposedly, he has a ranch near Eagle Pass, but spends most of his time in town showing off his pearl-handled pistols. Lots of people are afraid of him. You notice that most of the town's people got inside the stores when he rode by. He doesn't like Mexicans or Indians for that matter so I wanted us to be careful not to give him an excuse to shoot us."

Bat leaned back in his chair and took a sip of his coffee thinking it best to change the subject. "Ricardo, what's with all the bags of candles and red peppers?"

"The *candelabras* and the *ristas*? They're nice. Eh? They're decorations. Tomorrow's Christmas! Tonight, there's gonna be big festival in the plaza!"

"*Christmas*," remorsefully thought Bat, "*I wonder where Frank and Will are?*"

14 – Ricardo's Wife

Bat and Ricardo were well-rested and on their way to get their horses which had been freshly shod, thanks to Antonio. Bat picked up his bridle, but before he slipped the bit into Buck's mouth, he stopped and spoke to Ricardo, "From what I heard, not many people in Piedras Negras think much of Eagle Pass. How come?"

Ricardo leaned against the neck of his horse, buckled the ear strap of his horses bridle and said, "Eagle Pass was the first English-speaking town on the Rio Grande. People on the north side of the river used to speak Spanish, but Texas broke away from Mexico. Now all or most of the people there speak English. Also, there was a time when slave hunters hung out in Eagle Pass. Sometimes they snuck into town here searching for run-a-ways – we didn't think it was right. Guess our not liking Eagle Pass began for those reasons."

With the bridle on and Buck's saddle cinched tightly, Bat untied the halter rope from the railing and pressed Ricardo for more information. "You told me not to mention the word 'Kickapoo' when we were in Texas. Why?"

"It's a complicated story – like yours. I'll tell you along the way. Let's get started for Muzquiz. I want to see my children. We'll be about seven days on the road."

"I'm ready," replied Bat. "The way Buck is prancing, he is anxious to go too." As Bat and Ricardo started riding, Bat wondered, *"Ricardo said that he wants to see his children, but didn't say anything about his wife. He never has. Once he said that he used to have a Potawatomi wife. Guess they 'split the blanket.'"*

Shortly after leaving Piedras Negras, Ricardo began telling Bat more of where they were going. "Our last stop before we get to Muzquiz will be the Kickapoo village at El Nacimiento. It's now where most of the Kickapoo – and some Potawatomi are at. There used to be many Kickapoo and a few Potawatomi in Texas. Now, everybody's down here. They used to protect the white settlers up there from the Comanche and Apache. The white people liked them because of that."

"How come everybody came down here?" asked Bat.

Bat looked over at Ricardo who seemed to be lost in his thoughts so Bat repeated his question.

"Oh," Ricardo finally responded. "Lots of white settlers started coming into Texas. They wanted independence so they started fighting the Mexican army. The ones who wanted independence thought the Kickapoo would side with Mexico. As a result, the Kickapoo were considered to be on the wrong side and were no longer wanted by the white Texans. So, by the time your Civil War started, many Kickapoo were already in Mexico."

As Buck clip-clopped along, Bat silently thought about what Ricardo told him. After several minutes, Bat asked, "As far as you know, is that why the Kickapoo and Potawatomi who were at Dove Creek were headed for Mexico?"

"Yes," answered Ricardo. "After crossing the Rio Grande, they went to El Nacimiento – we'll stop there – so they could get far away from the border area – some Seminole and former black slaves used to live in El Nacimiento. The fight at Dove Creek made the Kickapoo hate Texas – made the Kickapoo want to get even. For several years after getting to Mexico, they carried out vengeance raids on the Texas settlements along the Rio Grande. I knew some of the warriors who went on the raids."

"One reason the Kickapoo and Potawatomi like it here is `cause the Mexican government leaves them alone and doesn't demand that they change their culture and traditions."

Bat started to explain, "It was different, especially for the Citizen Potawatomi who were sent to the Indian Territory up north. We . . ." He soon realized that Ricardo had grown quiet and had stopped listening. In a few days, Bat was to find out why.

******

Ricardo's despondency broke on the third day after leaving Piedras Negras.

"I used to go to Remolina after leaving Piedras Negras – it's straight west of here – about a day's ride," said Ricardo as he and Bat rode along the dusty road. Ricardo continued to look ahead, and Bat was not sure if his partner was speaking to him or to himself.

In an almost inaudible voice, Ricardo said, "I used to have lots of Kickapoo friends there – they're all gone from Remolina now. So is my wife. Most of the Kickapoo in Remolina were captured and taken to the Indian Territory. Stephanie, my dear wife was killed – shot in the head."

Bat firmly pulled on Buck's reins to stop him. Seeing that Bat had stopped, Ricardo reined his horse around to face him.

"I don't understand," Bat said in a most serious tone. "This is Mexico. Are you talkin' about the Indian Territory where I come from? You said that your wife was Potawatomi but that there were lots of Kickapoo in Remolina."

"I never talked to anyone about my wife's death – really murder – except to my parents and my sister, Veronica. In some ways it goes back to the killings at Dove Creek."

Bat sensed the need for Ricardo to keep on talking so he wisely did not interrupt him.

"The Kickapoo and Potawatomi who fled from Dove Creek – Stephanie was one of them – settled near El Nacimiento. She came to Muzquiz to trade when she was only sixteen. I met her there and immediately fell in love with her – she was so beautiful and charming. I went to her

74

village – El Nacimiento – and talked to her grandmother – her father was killed at Dove Creek – didn't know at the time what happened to her mother – into letting me marry her. She gave me two sons. Fortunately, they were in Muzquiz – with my mother and father – when the American soldiers came to Remolina where Stephanie was at."

Bat furrowed his brow and quizzically looked at Ricardo. "You just said 'the American soldiers came.' We're in Mexico. A few minutes ago you mentioned Dove Creek. What's the connection?"

Ricardo turned his horse around in the direction of Muzquiz and answered Bat as he continued on his ride home. "After the fight at Dove Creek, everyone quickly broke for Mexico. Unlike the Potawatomi – including Stephanie – the Kickapoo wanted revenge. They got it by raiding the Gringos along the Rio Grande. After several years, about four hundred American soldiers from Fort Clark – it's up by Eagle Pass – came across the Rio Grande one night and stormed into Remolina the next morning. They did what I said – killed a bunch of Kickapoo and taking many of them prisoners. Stephanie tried to protect a little Kickapoo girl, but both got shot."

"I would have been in Remolina when the soldiers came but I was invited to go on a hunt with most of the men and older boys. Stephanie urged me to go. We could have protected the village, but we had left about an hour earlier. We saw smoke coming from Remolina and knew there was trouble. Quickly, we forgot about the hunt and galloped back to Remolina. When we got back, Remolina was still burning –we were too late to do anything – that's when I saw Stephanie's body. It was horrible enough that she had been shot, but I could tell that she had been raped too."

Bat saw a look of deep hurt and anger come over Ricardo's face. He remembered that Ricardo stiffened when he saw a soldier ride by when they were passing through Eagle Pass. At the time, he didn't know why. Now he did.

Bat began recalling in his own mind the traumatic events that he had endured over the past two years: *"Mary's miserable death – I couldn't even find her grave after Pond Creek flooded – abandoned my sons after the marshal nearly hung me and then run me off."*

Bat's countenance and personality changed when he heard about Ricardo's tragic loss of Stephanie.

Back in Kansas – even in the Indian Territory – Bat recalled the lively and jubilant nature of his mother, Watchekee. Her characteristics had rubbed off on him. Now, sullenness pervaded his personality. Reaching back into his right saddle bag, Bat pulled out a flask of whiskey given to him by Antonio and drank until bitterness left his mind.

Only the clip-clop of two horses could be heard as Bat and Ricardo rode toward Muzquiz. They steeped in the silence of their own pent-up emotions.

Thirty minutes after Ricardo told Bat how Stephanie was killed, he said, "We'll go to El Nacimiento to see my friends there. I know a short-cut." He reined his horse off the dusty road running from Piedras Negras to Muzquiz and headed through the semi-desert accented by large patches of beaver-tail and ocotillo cacti. There was countless scrubby vegetation, all of which was unfamiliar to Bat.

Bat saw a range of mountains in the far distance. In a somewhat worried tone, he pointed to the mountains and asked a nonchalant Ricardo, "Do we have to cross over them?"

Ricardo grinned, "We need to ride through a little mountainous terrain but won't go over the mountains. They're the Sierra Hermosa de Santa Rosa. We'll stay on the east side of the mountains."

"Good!" said Bat who was trustingly trailing behind Ricardo.

15 – Broken Leg

Just before dark, Ricardo steered his horse onto a narrow, rocky trail and began ascending. Bat had no choice but to follow. Ricardo turned to tell Bat that they would stop for the night by a spring that was not far ahead. At the very moment he started to tell Bat about his plan, his horse suddenly reared and threw him. However, his right foot got caught in the saddle's stirrup. To avoid being dragged, Ricardo wrenched himself free, but an excruciating pain shot through his lower leg.

A black bear with her cub coming down the narrow trail had startled the horse. In its attempt to avoid the bear, Ricardo's horse jumped sideways after rearing, but stumbled off the path and bounced off a large boulder on the steep rocky hillside below the trail. Fortunately, Ricardo had freed himself from the stirrups before the horse fell off the trail.

Bat quickly dismounted Buck and was momentarily uncertain as what to do. Ahead of him was Ricardo writhing in pain and holding his leg. Coming from below the trail, was the shrill distress whinny of Ricardo's horse that was unsuccessfully trying to stand.

"MY LEG'S BROKEN!" shouted Ricardo. "CHECK MY HORSE. SHE'S HURT TOO!"

Bat scrambled down the slope and reached Ricardo's horse. One look at the horse told Bat that it also had a broken leg, a break that it had suffered when it hit the boulder. He yelled the bad news to Ricardo who had crawled to the edge of the trail and was now peering down at Bat and his horse.

Without hesitating, Bat took out his revolver and aimed it at the horse's head. "BLAM!" The horse's head bounced and instantly fell back to the ground. Bat looked up at Ricardo who nodded his head as a way of telling Bat that he had done the right thing.

Bat quietly holstered his pistol. He then retrieved Ricardo's saddle rifle and commenced stripping the tack off the dead horse. He had no trouble in getting the bridle free but the cinch strap was stuck under the weight of the horse's belly. Pulling hard, Bat freed the saddle after a few strong tugs on the cinch. Bat thought to himself as he plopped the saddle on the boulder that had hurt Ricardo's horse, *"I'll find this place and come back for the saddle. I need to figure out how to get Ricardo some help!"*

Bat climbed back up to the trail to look at Ricardo who was holding his right leg and wincing while looking skyward. "The bone's not sticking through, but your leg needs to be straightened out," said Bat. "Don't want you to have a limp like my mother did. Her leg got broken when she was young, and it healed a little crooked."

Ricardo paid no attention to what Bat had said because of the pain that was wracking his body.

Bat finally got Ricardo to look at him. He pulled out his hunting knife and handed it to Ricardo. "Put the dull side of the knife to the back of your throat and bite down hard on the blade. It's really gonna hurt when I pull on your leg!"

The ordeal of setting Ricardo's broken leg caused him to pass out. Bat's knife fell to the ground. Satisfied that Ricardo's leg was straight, Bat picked up the knife and began cutting four saplings to make a splint. He next cut and ripped long strips from the blanket in his bed roll. Ricardo's unconscious state, made it somewhat easy for Bat to affix the splint to Ricardo's injured lower leg. Next, Bat found a broken tree limb suitable for Ricardo to use as a crutch once he came to.

Ricardo regained consciousness after a few minutes and stared at Bat who said, "You mentioned there's a spring not far from here. I suggest we get to it and spend the night there. It's starting to get dark, but the full moon will give us some light.   Tomorrow morning, we'll go on to El Nacimiento if you can tell me how to get there."

Bat led Buck beside the injured Ricardo and asked, "Think you can get on? I'll lead Buck and walk. How far is the spring?"

"We can get to it in about ten minutes."
******

The spring and the open flat area around it was a welcome sight to Bat. He helped a groaning Ricardo to the ground and gave him a refreshing drink of the cool water gushing from the spring. Once, Bat had made Ricardo as comfortable as possible he started to get the tacos that Veronica had given them in Piedras Negras for their ride to Muzquiz. The tacos, though meager, would at least take away some of Bat's hunger. However, Ricardo, his body still racked in pain, waved off a taco when Bat offered it to him.

Bat only had taken two bites of his taco and was sipping his coffee when he heard the distinctive sound of approaching horses coming down the trail. Slowly, he put down his coffee mug and readied his saddle rifle while stepping away from the fire he had just started. He next pulled out his revolver and aimed it at the trail in the direction of the sounds he heard.

Three figures emerged from the dark shadows and stopped. Surprised to see Ricardo, who lay exposed because of the fire's illumination, and Bat's darkened figure, they began talking to each other. "They're deciding what to do," Bat whispered to Ricardo.

Bat had recognized and understood their language – Kickapoo.

The approaching men cautiously nudged their horses forward with their rifles posed to fight.

Ricardo not only recognized the language too but the men as well. He turned to Bat and gratefully, although in pain, said while squinting in the darkness, "We have friends! It's Kaw-kan-to-see! Mo-sha-she and Kick-ke-nic-quote are the ones with him. Hello! I'm Ricardo! My friend here is Bat! We need some help because I broke my leg!"

Because of the moon light, the Kickapoo men who were hunting had decided to ride down to the spring to camp. Had it been dark, they would have camped farther up the trail. Their decision to camp by the spring was fortuitous for Bat and Ricardo

Bat quickly realized that he and Ricardo not only had someone to help them, but that the men had three horses and a pack mule with them.

The Kickapoo, upon seeing that their friend, Ricardo, was badly hurt, unhesitatingly jumped off their horses; and tried to comfort him. Ricardo moved to greet the men and explain what had happened, but the movement set off a shock of pain up and down his leg causing him to stop talking as he slumped back onto his blanket.

Bat walked into the fire's light and over to his saddle bag. There he pulled out his flask of whiskey. Returning to Ricardo, he sat down and lifted Ricardo's head. Holding Ricardo's head in his hand, he said, "Take a good drink of this. It will dull the pain and help you get through the night."

After Ricardo took two big swigs, Bat extended the flask to the three Kickapoo men who had ridden into camp. One of the men waved off the offer, "No thanks. We're followers of the Kennekuk religion and stay away from alcohol." Bat recalled, *My mother once told me that she knew Kennekuk about the time she was married to Hubbard. She called Kennekuk a prophet.*" As recollections swirled through his head, Bat put the stopper back in the flask and put the flask next to Ricardo who by now was feeling the effects of the whiskey judging by the sounds of his deep breathing. Bat thought, *"Ricardo might be asleep now, but he'll need some more whiskey before the night is over."*

Throughout the night, Bat was awakened by Ricardo as his leg, now swollen and very painful, caused him to sleep fitfully. Not knowing what else to do, Bat offered Ricardo more whiskey each time to dull his pain.

When morning came, Bat held a brief meeting with the Kickapoo hunters to discuss the situation. Much to Bat's relief, the men readily agreed to let Bat use their pack mule to go back and retrieve Ricardo's saddle. Furthermore, the hunters told Bat that he could ride the mule to El Nacimiento, their village of five or so hundred people. This was good news to Bat. He now had transportation rather than having to walk and lead Buck carrying the injured Ricardo.

Bat was grateful that Ricardo now could get to El Nacimiento in a reasonable amount of time and mend. According to the Kickapoo hunters, their village was only a hard day's ride away. However, because of Ricardo's condition, the hunters told Bat that it would take until mid-afternoon of the second day before El Nacimiento could be reached.

Bat and the three hunters vainly tried to make Ricardo comfortable during the second night of camping. The pain in his broken leg still was very evident considering his restless sleep. Besides Ricardo's condition, there were sporadic sounds that made sleep nearly impossible for all the men.

Shortly after midnight, a piercing scream caused Bat to wake with a start. Just as he stood up, he recognized that it was the sound of a love-sick male bobcat in search of a mate and was not that of a woman screaming

"Ayee," said Kick-ke-nic-quote to Bat. "Have you ever tried that trick to get a woman?" The two other hunters chuckled as they turned over and began going back to sleep.

Groggy, Ricardo heard the comment and thought, *"Only if I felt good enough so I could tell them how Bat lost his wife."*

A period of quietness descended over the camp for the next two hours. When everything seemed peaceful, a slight rustling of leaves caused the hunters to open their eyes and reach for their rifles. They had been asleep but still alert enough hoping yet to have a successful hunt. Bat, who had been awake because of Ricardo's discomfort, quietly asked Kaw-kan-to-see, "What is it?"

Kaw-kan-to-see answered in a hushed voice, "Javelinas. They're next to the creek. Look over there."

Bat strained his eyes. Enough moonlight filtered through the canopy of the boughs of the abundant Ponderosa Pines that he was able to make out three, darkish pig-like bodies. The animals' snouts rippled the ripened seed heads of grasses. Faint munching sounds indicated that the javelinas were enjoying a late-night meal.

"BLAM!" Bat flinched, and all of the horses and the mule jumped in spite of their hobbles. Ricardo, still subdued by the last drink of whiskey, scarcely moved. Kaw-kan-to-see, the lead hunter, barely had nodded his head when three simultaneous shots from the hunters' guns tore into the small herd of javelinas. Two of the javelinas fell by the creek. The third javelina, which partially had been shielded by one of the other wild pigs, let out a loud squeal and started running up hill although seriously wounded. Five piglets, which the hunters and Bat had not detected, chased after her.

Kaw-kan-to-see turned to his partners and softly said, "At least, we'll have some meat to take back. Get the two javelinas that we shot, drag them back, and hang them in the tree over there. We'll skin them in the morning."

Bat opened his eyes at the first hint of daybreak and expected to see the suspended carcasses of the javelinas that had been shot only hours earlier. Instead, he saw two skin-wrapped bundles. The hunters already had skinned and butchered their kill, but there were only two Kickapoo men still in camp.

"Where is Mo-sha-she?" inquired Bat.

Kaw-kan-to-see merely pointed upstream with pursed lips. The gesture by Kaw-kan-to-see told Bat that the missing man was tracking the wounded javelina.

Just then, everyone heard a twig break. Turning toward the direction of the sound, Mo-sha-she appeared with a dead javelina sow slung over his shoulders.

"Was it hard to track her?" asked Bat.

"No," replied Mo-sha-she, "she left a blood trail. I found her not far up the creek. So had a bobcat – probably the same one we heard last night. It had eaten part of the javelina and had covered up the rest of her carcass with needles and leaves."

Kaw-kan-to-see, who had strolled over to the creek's edge, crouched down and said, "A larger cat also paid our camp a visit." He turned to look at Bat and the other hunters and motioned for them to come and see the tracks he had spotted. Once the men were around him, Kaw-kan-to-see pointed at a track with his finger and said, "Jaguar. Not many of them around here. – The blood from the javelinas we shot must have attracted it."

"Ohoo," moaned Ricardo. His groaning broke up the excitement of having a formidable night visitor. Soon everyone was busy fixing breakfast and getting ready to leave camp. Bat took it on himself to look after Ricardo and help him get on Buck so they could get to El Nacimiento.

16 – Kickapoo Village

Bat trusted the Kickapoo hunters, but was at their mercy as the group descended a narrow rocky trail on the eastern side of the Sierra Hermosa de Santa Rosa. Along the way, Bat frequently thought, *"I hope they know where they're going. Shouldn't we get to El Nacimiento pretty soon?"* Ricardo knew the way to the Kickapoo's isolated village in northern Mexico, but he was in no condition to tell Bat anything or assure him that they were being guided in the right direction.

Ricardo's mishap had occurred in the pines and scrub oaks. Slowly the woody montane vegetation gave way to the brushy semi-desert flora of the foothills.

A short climb to the top of one foothills occurred just when Bat's uncertainties began to peak. When the crest of the hill was reached, Kaw-kan-to-see stopped the procession. He turned his horse around and motioned for Bat to join him.

"What now?" Bat said to himself as he urged his mule forward while leading Buck who was carrying Ricardo.

"I want you to see our village from this hill," said Kaw-kan-to-see. In order to see the same view, he backed up his horse and reined it around."

Bat's jaw dropped as he looked at the village in the extensive valley below – El Nacimiento – wigwams – lots of them. *"My mother,"* he recalled, *"told me that she once lived in one. She also said that she her Kickapoo friends who used to live in Danville, Illinois, lived in them too."*

The wigwams that Bat saw seemingly were randomly scattered. The log cabins and frame houses that he left behind in Kansas and the Indian Territory were either isolated or laid out geometrically. A clear-water river visibly formed the village's eastern edge. The wigwams, each covered with woven cattail mats, reflected like jewels in the afternoon sun. Wisps of smoke rose from each dwelling. To Bat, the wisps seemed to slowly dance in the air.

Ricardo managed to lift his head to see the village himself. In a feeble voice, he said, "Bat, we made it."

Kaw-kan-to-see's twelve-year-old son, Pah-ko-tah, had been keeping a lookout for the return of the hunting party. When he spotted riders on the trail, he led his horse to tree stump and squirmed onto the horse's back while holding the reins. Once astride his horse, he quickly rode bareback from the village and up the hill to greet his father and the other men. He knew that his father and two other hunters had left on three horses and one pack mule. However, he easily counted five men, each on a horse plus one on the mule. Eager to find out who was with the hunting party, Pah-ko-tah urged his horse to go fast and lunged up the hill.

As he reined his horse to a halt, he smiled and greeted his father. "How was the hunting?" he asked.

Kaw-kan-to-see replied, "We only got three javelinas. We hoped to get a bear and some deer, but we had to come home early. We'll go again."

"How come you came back so soon?" asked Pah-ko-tah. Just as he asked why the hunt was so short, the lad glanced at Bat and Ricardo who were on their mounts beside Kaw-kan-to-see. Pah-ko-tah seemed to recognize Ricardo. The presence of Ricardo and the stranger next to him explained the additional men. Still in his mind he wondered, *"What did Ricardo and his friend have to do with the hunt?"* While Pah-ko-tah was still trying to understand why the hunt was so short, his horse danced around to the other side of his father's horse. There, Pah-ko-tah's gaze caught the splint on Ricardo's leg.

Pah-ko-tah looked over at his father. Soon, an animated discussion between the two of them was underway. Gesturing, Kaw-kan-to-see explained how Ricardo got hurt and what needed to be done now. Pah-ko-tah listened intently to the instructions that his father gave him. The boy took another quick look at Ricardo's leg and without saying another word, turned his horse around and raced down to the village.

Ricardo looked at Bat and said, "I couldn't ride that fast down a hill like that even if my leg wasn't broken."

Bat replied, "Don't worry. We'll get you down there. Let Buck do the work. He'll probably lower his haunches and slide on the loose rocks. Just lean back and stay in the saddle. We'll go slow."

17 – *El Toro*

Ricardo was taken to Kaw-kan-to-see's wigwam after he and Bat arrived in El Nacimiento. Having been alerted by Pah-ko-tah, Kaw-kan-to-see's wife, Pa-na-tho, immediately began to take care of him. She directed the hunters to lay Ricardo on a bed woven from thin willow stems and covered with the skins of a bear and three deer. Although Ricardo was worn out from his ordeal, Pa-na-tho made him eat the evening meal that she already had cooked, corn pones and a hot dish of pork and squash. Once, Pa-na-tho was satisfied that Ricardo was well-fed, she allowed him to drift into a deep slumber.

The next morning, Bat threw back the blanket doorway of Kaw-kan-to-see's wigwam to see how Ricardo was doing. Once, Bat's eyes adjusted to the darkness, he saw that Ricardo was fast asleep – so he thought. Instead, Ricardo opened his eyes and threw back his blanket. Next he said, "Bat? Is that you? I've got to pee!"

Humored by the situation, Bat said, "Not here! I'll get your crutch and help you get to the edge of the village."

******

A month later on the habitual morning outing while struggling up the river bank next to the Kickapoo village and nearly exhausted, Ricardo asked, "Bat, can you do me a favor?"

"Of course!" replied Bat.

"We've been here about a month. I need to get to Muzquiz to see my boys, Alfredo and Tomas. They and their grandparents – my mother and father – they live with them – expect me in about this time each year, but I don't have a horse. Besides that, even though my leg is getting stronger, it still isn't strong enough for me to ride to Muzquiz."

"Sounds like you need two favors – gettin' you a horse and seein' your boys to let them know you'll be home later."

Bat went silent at the thought of seeing Ricardo's sons. In his own mind he wondered, *"How are Frank and Will? Do Kate and Joe know why I left? I hope they're takin' good care of my boys."*

Ricardo noticed that Bat was in a far away stare and asked, "What's wrong?"

"Nothin'" answered Bat as he snatched off a stem of dry grass. He shook his head to get his mind off Frank and Will. "I should be able to get you a horse – might have to do some breakin' for people in the village – but I can't do nothin' 'bout your leg. Guess that means I should go on to Muzquiz without you. When do you think you'll be strong enough to get home?"

"I hope in about two weeks – I'd be grateful if I can go sooner – won't be able to stay long because it'll be about time to go back and find some work driving a herd to Kansas" replied Ricardo. Bat glanced at Ricardo and saw sorrow and frustration in his eyes.

******

After breakfast in early February, Bat and Kaw-kan-to-see rode out to see the Kickapoo's horse herd that was grazing east of the river that ran by the village. "See that black stallion over there – the one by itself? No one has been able to ride him," said Kaw-kan-to-see.

"If I break him to ride, can I give him to Ricardo?" asked Bat.

"You can try. Yes, I've been thinking about Ricardo. He needs a horse," replied Kaw-kan-to-see. Teasingly, he looked at Bat and repeated "You can try."

Later in morning, Bat and Kaw-kan-to-see were joined by Mo-sha-she for the single purpose of helping Bat catch the stallion that couldn't be ridden. Soon they lassoed him with two lariats. Kaw-kan-to-see and Mo-sha-she jumped off their horses after roping the stallion and their feet sent up dust clouds as the two men were dragged along in an attempt to slow down and tire the wild horse.

"Tie 'em to the Palo Verde over there!" shouted Bat. "Snug 'em up so he can't move around much!"

Kaw-kan-to-see and Mo-sha-she warily did as instructed so they wouldn't get kicked or bitten.

By now, several other men and boys had waded across the river to watch Bat try and ride the stallion.

Bat looked over his shoulder and said to Kaw-kan-to-see, "Tell 'em to go back to the village! I don't need a crowd. They'll make the horse nervous."

Kaw-kan-to-see shrugged his shoulders and then waved in the direction of the village. He was telling the onlookers to go back. Although muttering, everyone went back across the river, but hunkered down on the river's bank. They still watched but at a distance.

"I'd like to work with the horse alone now that he's tied up and tired," said Bat looking at Kaw-kan-to-see and Mo-sha-she. In a disappointed fashion, they joined the others who had left moments earlier.

Bat then turned to the stallion and in a soft, calming voice said, "Now it's just you and me. You need a name – how 'bout Toro? You're black like some of the bulls I've seen 'round here. You think you're tough like *El Toro*, but you're really not."

Ever so slowly and gently, Bat introduced Toro to the tack – bridle, saddle blanket, saddle – by letting the horse smell each item. By mid- afternoon, Bat had Toro calm enough to put a saddle on him without Toro throwing his head back and rearing up.

Sitting on the far side of the stream, Kaw-kan-to-see grinned and looked at Mo-sha-she. He said with a glint in his eyes, "If Bat gets on that horse, get ready for some real bucking. The women will enjoy pulling cactus spines out of his rear." Kaw-kan-to-see patted his buttocks, causing Mo-sha-she to laugh.

To their utter amazement, the black stallion let Bat get on. Gently urging Toro forward, Bat headed for the river. As the horse and rider neared the stream, everyone, including Kaw-kan-to-see and Mo-sha-she, hastily retreated to the safety of the village.

Bat nervously coaxed Toro to cross the river. When the two of them finally got across, Bat reined Toro in the direction of Pa-na-tho's wigwam. Pa-na-tho looked up from the ramada where she had started cooking the evening meal. Afraid of the black stallion, she uttered a fearful sound, tripped, got back up, and fled into her wigwam.

Ricardo was awakened by the commotion and limped outside just as Bat and Toro got to the lodge.

Bat was grinning. "I got you a good horse," he said. "Tomorrow, I'll work two more horses and then be on my way come the next day to see your boys in Muzquiz." Patting Toro on the neck, Bat explained, "I'll leave Buck with you and take Toro with me."

"Toro?" smiled Ricardo.

"Yes, Toro – he's black and strong like a bull. Toro still might want to throw a rider. I don't know yet. Anyway, I don't want you on him just yet. Buck is gentle and will get you to Muzquiz without any problems when you are healed enough to ride. I figure that I can get Toro really well-trained goin' to Muzquiz. Maybe you knowin' that you can have Toro there will speed up your mendin'."

******

Bat and Ricardo sat near the breakfast fire the next morning in front of Kaw-kan-to-see's and Pa-na-tho's wigwam. They had just finished their breakfast of toasted corn and beans. Bat fanned the smoke away from his face and asked Ricardo, "How long will it take me to ride to Muzquiz?" In just a few minutes, Bat would be leaving to find Ricardo's children.

"Take the trail that goes southeast . . ." Ricardo started to say but was uncharacteristically interrupted by Bat.

"I know the direction, but how long?"

"*He's anxious*," thought Ricardo. "*Don't blame him.*" Finally, Ricardo held up two fingers and said, "Two – maybe three day's ride. When you start seeing wattle and daub jacales near the trail, you'll know you're only about three kilometers away. My cousin and his wife live in the first jacal that you'll see on the right side of the trail. He used to be a drover, like me, until he got bucked off his horse and hurt his back." In somewhat of a trance, Ricardo mused, "*There probably will be a pig and a chicken or two standing near their door waiting for some scraps.*"

18 – Arrival in Muzquiz

Bat said with a lump in his throat, *"Bama pi, Mgwetch."* Everyone understood. Mounting Toro, Bat tipped his hat and looked at Ricardo. "See you in Muzquiz."

"Wait!" said Pa-na-tho as she scurried back into her wigwam and quickly came back outside. "You will need this!" Reaching up to Bat, she handed him a small sack of dried corn mixed with dried venison. "It will make good soup." Bat merely nodded his head in gratitude. He then turned Toro around and without saying anything left El Nacimiento, the Kickapoo village.

Bat soon realized that he was alone and had no one to talk to. He and Ricardo had been together ever since meeting each other along the Red River that separated Texas from the Indian Territory. Nearly five months had passed. As Bat slowly made his way along the trail to Muzquiz, his thoughts turned to his lost life, *"Mary, why did you have to die – would it have been different if we'd stayed in Kansas? How are Frank and Will? I still have to wait five more years before I can go back to the Reservation and see them. Maybe the marshal's dead by now – naw, I can't chance it – don't want to get strung up like those two horse thieves."*

"WAIT UP!"

Bat pulled on the reins and stopped Toro. He had been on the rocky and dirt wagon road that led from El Nacimiento for only about ten minutes. Turning in his saddle and looking backwards, he couldn't believe who he heard and saw. It was Ricardo. He had Buck at a full gallop. He might as well have been riding bareback because only his left foot was in a stirrup. His right leg, still in splints, hung down. Gripping the saddle horn tightly with his left hand, he brought Buck to a halt next to Bat and Toro.

Ricardo patted the thigh of his right leg as Buck snorted and breathed heavily and said to Bat, "I couldn't stay in El Nacimiento any longer and wait for this thing to get stronger. It still hurts, especially after riding hard to catch up with you, but I need to see Alfredo and Tomas – haven't seen them in nearly a year. My leg can heal in Muzquiz as well as lying around in Pa-na-tho's wigwam. I just need to get there."

Bat grinned and nodded his head to acknowledge that he understood Ricardo's concern. But as Toro danced around and threw his head up nervously, Bat glanced at Ricardo's leg and said, "Sure you can make it."

Though grimacing, Ricardo said, "I got on Buck and made it this far – didn't I?"

******

Bat cast benign glances at Ricardo as they rode along to see how his friend was holding up. Based on the countenance of Ricardo's face and his general body posture toward the end of the third day of the journey, Bat sensed that they were getting close to where Ricardo's sons were living with his parents. Just one kilometer northwest of Muzquiz, Ricardo was hunched in his saddle, trying unsuccessfully to conceal the ache in his right leg. Now, he was almost gleeful.

It was obvious to Bat that he and Ricardo finally had arrived in Muzquiz, a community built in a rocky, semi-arid area bisected by several streams. They had passed numerous jacals on the northwest side of the little town. Dusty side streets branched rather haphazardly from the street that Bat and Ricardo now found themselves riding on. Coming to the plaza marking the center of Muzquiz, Ricardo said, "Bat, we'll turn left at the next corner."

The turn led the weary pair of travelers a short distance east along a twisting road. In front of a large, white adobe-style *casa* (house), Ricardo stopped. He held up his hand and said to Bat, "We're here!" The *casa's* yard

contrasted to what Bat had seen in El Nacimiento. The yard
he now viewed was filled with numerous trees and flowering
plants of varying shapes. The areas immediately surrounding
the wigwams in El Nacimiento were void of any vegetation.

"What's with all the plants?" asked Bat.

"My mother likes them," responded Ricardo as he
gently nudged Buck forward.   "I'm sure she will tell you
what each plant is. Right now, I want to see Alfredo and
Tomas!"

Before Bat and Ricardo could enter the yard, a burro
pulling a cart full of charcoal pulled in front of them.
Following Ricardo's lead, Bat stepped his horse back to
allow the cart to pass. In a respectful way, Ricardo tipped his
hat at the slight, gray-haired man driving the cart. The man
quickly jerked his burro to a stop. He hopped off the cart and
walked over to Ricardo. Looking up at Ricardo, he smiled
and warmly shook his hand. A short but lively conversation
ensued, part of which involved the splints on Ricardo's right
leg.

After the man climbed back onto his cart and headed
toward the *casa*, Bat asked Ricardo, "Who's that?"

"He's my father's oldest brother. Let's follow him.
He'll take us to the back of the *casa* where my mother does
her cooking.   Considering the lateness of the day, she's
probably working on supper."

"Henrico, I'm glad that you finally came with my
charcoal! Now I can finish my cooking! I was starting to get
worried," said Ricardo's mother, Mercedes, a gray-haired
woman in her late fifties, short but plump. Although she had
her back to Henrico when he arrived, his cart's squeaking
wheels told her that he had come. Pushing and shoving, she
slapped and patted the tortilla dough as if she were mad at it.

Taking some of the charcoal that Henrico had
brought, she started a fire under her earthen oven. Still, she
did not see the others who had arrived behind him. She then
picked up a large wooden spoon and started to stir a pot of
black beans in a pot over another fire.

Mercedes started to turn and scold Henrico for his usual delivery tardiness. She dropped her mixing spoon when Ricardo, who had been sitting atop Buck, said, "Mother, where's Alfredo and Tomas?"

Speechless at first, she turned and stood staring at Ricardo. Tears came to her eyes. Ricardo dismounted and hugged his mother who rushed to him. While still embracing her son, she shouted "JOSÈ, COME AND SEE WHO'S HOME!" José, Ricardo's father, was sleeping in his hammock, which was slung between two walnut trees growing by the far corner of the *casa*. Just as Mercedes called for her husband, she noticed the splints on Ricardo's leg. "What happened?" she asked as both hands came up to her face. She was motionless and could see that her son was in pain as he faced her.

"I'll explain later – oh, this is my friend Bat – where are my sons?" responded Ricardo who was looking past his mother trying to spot Alfredo and Tomas.

"I sent them to look for some chicken eggs about ten minutes ago. They probably got to playing with the goats," said Mercedes whose eyes had become fixed on her son's leg.

José finally woke up and nearly fell to the ground from the hammock when he saw Ricardo. Henrico and Bat stood back as he semi-ran by to greet his son.

After but a few minutes, Ricardo affectionately grasped his mother by her shoulders and then said, "Excuse me mother, I'm gonna find my boys." He waved for Bat to join him and limped toward the goat pasture.

Bat got off Toro and tied him and Buck to a nearby hitching post. Giving Buck a playful swat on the horse's haunches, he then hurried to catch up with Ricardo. His mind was flooded with thoughts of his own sons, Frank and Will, as he walked along with Ricardo.

A basket with two eggs told Ricardo and Bat that the boys were close by. It predictably was by the gate to the goat pasture.

What was to be a joyous moment when Ricardo saw his sons was a moment of deep disappointment. To Alfredo and Tomas, their father was a stranger. During Ricardo's long absence, they had forgotten their father and didn't recognize him.

19 – Drover on the Chisholm Trail

A few weeks later when rays of the morning sun began filtering into the bedroom they shared, Bat heard Ricardo say, "Want to be a drover? You handle horses good – ever work with cattle?"

"I used to herd the milk cows and steers my family had in Louisville, Kansas – more like bringin' 'em in and movin' 'em from one pasture to another than actually herdin' 'em. Back in the Indian Territory – before I was run off the Potawatomi Reservation – I had started to develop a cattle business – did some actual herdin' then. Also, we did some herdin' comin' down here. – Remember? Why do you ask?" replied Bat as he pulled on his boots.

Life in Muzquiz had been relaxing. During the past couple of months while Ricardo's leg healed, Bat helped repair the outbuildings and do the other work that Ricardo normally would have done when he came home. José contemplated what needed to be done in the comfort of his hammock before and after his afternoon siestas. When the opportunity availed, Mercedes put Bat to work in her flower gardens.

One morning, Ricardo watched Bat get on his last boot and said, "Well, I'll be heading north to Texas tomorrow morning to get a herd of longhorns and take 'em up the Chisholm Trail to Abilene, Kansas. I thought you might want to help me. Some days are pretty tough. They can be dangerous too – especially going across river crossings and when cattle rustlers show up – not to mention storms – lightning strikes can trigger a stampede. The pay isn't too good but there isn't much to spend it on. Mostly, I like the solitude and food from the chuck wagon. After I get my herd to Abilene, I just turn around and come back here. You're welcome to do the same."

"Let me think about it," replied Bat as he stood up and gazed hypnotically out the bedroom window.

"What are you looking at?" curiously asked Ricardo.

"Alfredo and Tomas – they're chasin' a rooster with sticks. I remember doin' the same thing when I was small."

"Where was that?"

"Along the Missouri River – I heard my mother and father refer to the area as Council Bluffs."

As Bat watched the frolicking of Ricardo's sons, thoughts of Frank and Will surfaced in his mind. *"I hope they're healthy and with Kate."*

Misty-eyed, Bat turned from the window and looking at Ricardo said, "Yep." He then went outside to get breakfast.

Ricardo was confused. *"How could driving a herd cause him to get all teary-eyed?"*

******

Bat looked at the store fronts of Eagle Pass as he and Ricardo headed north and asked, "Where and how're we gonna get a herd to take to Abilene?"

"Don't worry," replied Ricardo. "My only concern now is getting through this place before John Fisher comes riding in and looking for trouble." *"This town used to be nothing but a trading post,"* surfaced in his thoughts again. Ricardo had another concern that he chose not to talk to Bat about it again. It was too personal and an emotional one, especially if he saw a soldier. Anyone from Fort Duncan brought back memories of the violation and death of his innocent wife.

"There ain't many steers around here. The only ones I've seen are headin' south – to Mexico," said Bat who was momentarily distracted by a drunk being tossed out of a saloon. "It's too early for that kind of stuff," he muttered to himself

"We need to ride further north – probably starting around the Dove Creek area. There, we'll find plenty of ranchers who want to get their herds to market," assured Ricardo. "We'll start by asking Tankersley, the guy we did some work for."

"You mean Richard Tankersley?"

"Yes. He'll probably have some more steers ready to be driven. Also, we might get several smaller herds from neighboring ranchers and make one big herd. All we'll need is a head count from each rancher. Tankersley trusts me and he'll put in a good word for me."

"While we are up there, I'll get some other drovers to help us. I know who I want if we get our herd around Dove Creek. We'll need about ten other men. With the two of us, we'll have twelve drovers. I figure about one drover for each one-hundred steers. One of them will know of a good cook who has a chuck wagon. The cook usually will get his own assistant – someone who's too young to be a drover."

Bat's and Ricardo's ride north to get or assemble a herd for the drive to Kansas was uneventful. They had outfitted their journey by securing a pack horse in Piedras Negras. It was loaded with camping supplies and the food they would need before securing a chuck wagon on the drive itself. The food was a welcome contribution from Ricardo's sister, Veronica, and her husband. Their hospitality was enjoyed by Bat and Ricardo the night before crossing the Rio Grande and entering Texas.

******

"Need a helping hand?" asked Ricardo.

Ricardo's voice surprised Richard Tankersley, who was in his corral breaking a mare that had foaled three weeks earlier.

"Let my friend, Bat, work with her. He knows what to do and can get on her in no time. While he breaks her, I want to talk to you."

"No problem. Bat, she's all yours!"

Tankersley crawled through the corral's fence to where Ricardo now was standing and asked him, "What's up?"

Ricardo knew that Tankersley didn't want any small talk so he got right down to business. "Do you have any steers ready to be driven up to Abilene?"

"Seven hundred and fifty-three."

"I was hoping for about twelve hundred," responded Ricardo as he took a long drag on his pipe.

"You'all want twelve hundred?"

"Yep."

"Tomorrow, let's ride into San Angelo. A bunch of guys and me will be in a meetin' there. Bet we can get you 'all some more steers. I know that some of my neighbors are anxious about getting their stock taken to market. You 'all came at the right time," said Tankersley. "Hey! Look at Bat. He's already standing next to her, and she's not pulling at the rope to get away!"

******

Two days later, Ricardo and Bat along with ten others slowly rode around a milling herd of twelve hundred and eleven longhorns. Most were steers but a few cows with older calves were in the count.

Bat rode over to Ricardo and asked "What're we waitin' for?"

Straining his eyes, Ricardo calmly said, "The chuck wagon. While we're waiting – there it comes – let me say that our worst river crossing will come in about three weeks. It's the South Canadian. It's bad for quicksand. Most of the drovers know about it, but I'll talk about it when we come to the river."

Seeing a canvas-topped wagon on the road leading up to Tankersley's ranch, Ricardo whistled and waved his arm to get the attention of the other men. "Bat, you take the left rear today. Make sure there're no stragglers! It'll get dusty, but I'll move you up tomorrow"

"MOVE `EM OUT!" barked Ricardo.

Slowly, the long, northward drive from Dove Creek, Texas, to Abilene, Kansas, began.

******

Bat was filled with many thoughts. First, there was the excitement of the drive itself. Another was the prospect of seeing his sons. The latter thought kept churning through his mind, but the feeling was cancelled by a lingering fear.

He knew that the drive eventually would be on the Chisholm Trail and its northern route would go through the heart of the Indian Territory. *"When it crosses the South Canadian River, I'll only be about a day's ride west of where my sons, Frank and Will, should be living with my sister Kate and Joe. Maybe, I'll have a chance to see my boys,"* he thought.

However, his fear of running into Ed Trumball, the U.S. Marshal, overrode his lingering desire to see his sons. After all, it was Trumball who forced him to watch the two horse thieves get lynched and threatened to hang him if he was found in the area during the next seven years. Thoughts about a family reunion soon were supplanted by the dust thrown up by the herd that Bat was following and the constant chasing of straggling steers.

******

"Mexican food for Gringo food," muttered Ricardo as he ate in the evening after crossing the Red River, the boundary between Texas and the Indian Territory.

"How's that?" asked Bat who as sitting beside him.

"Rice and beans for pork and beans!"

The quip made both men chuckle.

Bat then sopped up the last of his pork and beans with a piece of sour dough bread and slurped his coffee. "The drive up through Texas seemed to go pretty smooth," he said.

"Yes, if you'll excuse me, I need to take a ride around the cattle. Hopefully, they're done grazing. All of them should be bedding down soon and chewing their cuds."

******

Bat threw out his bed roll and laid back. Overhead in the clear, dark sky, he saw only a myriad of twinkling stars. It was a peaceful moment. He knew his rest would end when his turn to monitor the herd came.

Other drovers were engaged in a quiet conversation when Ricardo slowly rode in. The words of "Morales – raid – Kickapoo" caused him to stop. Jeremy, the one drover who he didn't know when the drive started near Dove Creek, was the man Ricardo heard talking.

Riding over to where Jeremy had settled in for the night, Ricardo dismounted Toro and pulled out his revolver. Grabbing Jeremy by the front of his long johns and jerking him, he yelled, "GET UP!"

The sudden change in Ricardo's tenor startled the whole camp, especially Jeremy.

"Were you soldiering at Fort Clark in 1872?"

"Yes! Why . . . . ?"

As Ricardo continued to shake a terrified Jeremy, he said, "I heard you say something about the Kickapoo in Morales!"

"Yes! We raided them 'cause they were causin' problems along the border!"

Ricardo cocked his revolver and aimed it at the face of Jeremy. "My wife was visiting friends in Morales! SHE WAS RAPED AND SHOT DURING YOUR SO-CALLED RAID!"

"I-I-I-I didn't kill or hurt any women – only some older men and boys who were shootin' at us!" cried Jeremy who slumped down and began pleading for mercy.

"He's telling the truth!" said Mark Luther who stepped forward. Mark was the drover whom Ricardo had known the longest and one whom he trusted. "Please don't shoot him! You'll spook the whole herd and stampede it."

Standing over Jeremy, Ricardo looked at Mark and asked "How do you know?"

"He talked to me 'bout the raid a year ago. Because of the raid, he quit the cavalry. Besides, the one who raped and shot the woman – had to be your wife – he got court martialed and hung."

Still glaring at and keeping his pistol trained on him, Ricardo growled, "GET YOUR CLOTHES AND GET OUT OF HERE!"

Quickly, Jeremy did as he was told. Under the watchful eye of Ricardo, he saddled his horse and disappeared.

As soon as he was gone, Ricardo holstered his pistol and turned to his men. Calmly, he said, "We still got a herd to get to Abilene. Some of you got a watch tonight so let's get settled back down."

******

Several days later, Bat rode over to Ricardo to talk about the cattle drive as it neared the South Canadian River and said, "Ricardo, we can't be too far from the South Canadian. Think we can get across it before nightfall?"

"That's my plan," answered Ricardo. He smiled and said, "We'd better. That's where we are to meet the chuck wagon!"

Both men laughed and patted their stomachs.

"Say, Ricardo, since you got rid of Jeremy some of the men have been grumblin' 'bout the extra work they got to do – especially the longer night watches and havin' to round up more strays. Know what I mean?"

"Yes. I've learned to expect the loss of a man here and there," said Ricardo as he casually turned a steer back into the moving herd.

"I think I can get someone to help us at least until we get into Kansas," commented Bat.

"Who?"

"Remember the time we met?" asked Bat.

"Sure do. I thought you were a Mexican because of your brown skin and black mustache."

"Well," said Bat, "I spent the previous year with a Chickasaw man and his son. The son, Benjamin Arkeketa, is old enough to help us and has his own horse. I know. I gave it to him. He'll probably be glad to get some work. He doesn't live too far from here. I can be back with him before we have to cross the South Canadian."

"Go get him then."

Neither Bat nor Ricardo had seen the rider approaching from the north. "Afternoon," the stranger said as he rode up to Ricardo. The greeting startled Ricardo. "I saw your herd coming and decided to stop and see it. I'm Marshal Trumball – Ed Trumball – just returning from havin' met the new commandant up at Fort Reno." Ricardo easily saw the reflection on the marshal's badge. "Say, who's the trail boss of this here herd?"

"That's me," answered Ricardo. Hearing the stranger identify himself as Marshal Trumball put him on edge. Hiding his concern, Ricardo asked himself, *"What if he finds that Bat's with us?"*

Trumball stared at the man riding northwest and asked Ricardo, "Mind telling me who just rode off?"

Pointing at the galloping Bat, Ricardo said "Him? He's my cousin, José Nieto. We're both from Muzquiz, Mexico. We drove every year."

"If he's your cousin from Mexico, why's he ridin' away like he knows where he's goin'?" asked a suspicious Marshal Trumball.

As he winked, Ricardo leaned over and said, "He's got a Chickasaw woman friend a few miles from here. Know what I mean?"

Marshal Trumball shrugged his shoulders and pursed his lips not realizing who he had actually seen. He tipped his hat as he started to ride away and said, "Your cousin reminds me of someone I dealt with about two years ago – have a good day."

"It's a good thing me and Bat switched horses this morning. The marshal might've recognized him if he'd been riding Buck," Ricardo thought. He then made his way to the west side of the herd so he could more easily scan the horizon and watch for Bat's return. Finally, one mile from the South Canadian River crossing, he spotted Bat and a rider with him. *"He must have gotten that Chickasaw boy to come and join us. Good,"* he thought and rode out to meet Bat.

A short distance from the crossing, Ricardo told Bat that Trumball was in the area. Hearing the name Trumball, caused Bat to nervously and warily look around.

"Bat, the safest place for you is on the north side of the river," said Ricardo.

"Oh! Ricardo, this is Benjamin Arkeketa. Benjamin, this is Ricardo Pacheco. Ricardo's the trail boss."

After the handshakes and exchange of greetings, Benjamin, who knew about Bat's troubles with Trumball, said, "Bat, I know a place upstream where there is no quicksand. Me and you can cross there and then double back and meet the herd when it crosses the river. We'll hide in a willow thicket along the north bank until we know it's safe."

Having seen Trumball ride south several miles back, Ricardo agreed with Benjamin's idea and rode back to the herd to help get it across the river.

Ricardo shouted instructions to his men when he returned to the moving mass of longhorns, "MARK, YOU AND JACK, KEEP THE HERD PUSHED TOWARD THE CROSSING! SEVERAL OF YOU OTHERS, FAN OUT AND FORM A FUNNEL! DON'T LET ANY STEERS BREAK THROUGH – KEEP 'EM MOVING TOWARD THE RIVER. A COUPLE OF US, ME AND JASON, WILL GET TO THE REAR OF THE HERD AND START SHOOTING INTO THE AIR AND HOLLERING. THE NOISE WILL MOVE THE HERD AWAY FROM US AND TOWARD THE RIVER. WHEN THE HERD STARTS

MOVING, FIRE YOUR GUNS TOO SO THE HERD STAYS BUNCHED. MAKE LOTS OF NOISE. WE'VE DONE THIS BEFORE, SO YOU KNOW WHAT TO DO! COME ON. JASON. LET'S GET 'EM GOING!"

The dangers of the South Canadian River soon were realized. Five steers were lost when they broke away from the herd while crossing the river and sank in the river's infamous quicksand. All of the drovers, including Ricardo, helplessly stood by and watched as the steers disappeared.

The averted encounter with Marshal Trumball fueled Bat's fears of going back to see Frank and Will. As the herd passed by the Cheyenne Agency Wagon Road, a road that led east to the Citizen Potawatomi Reservation and nearly to the cabin that he and Mary had been building, Bat once again was tempted to see his sons. However, the haunting fear of being lynched and the memory of the twitching feet prevailed.

20 – It's Bat – Bat's Back!

Muzquiz, Mexico, to Abilene, Kansas, and back to Muzquiz. Bat spent the next five years as a drover and became well-acquainted with Texas cattlemen and the Chisholm Trail. While in Mexico, he split his time working for Ricardo's father and visiting Kickapoo and Potawatomi friends living in their reclusive village at El Nacimiento.

It wasn't an ideal arrangement because of the emotions that weighed on Bat. Every time he came to the juncture of the Chisholm Trail and the Cheyenne Agency Wagon Road, he was tempted to leave the cattle drive and find his boys on the reservation. Each time, he was held back by the fear of being caught and hung by Marshal Trumball. Little did he know that the one he feared had died of a broken neck suffered when his run-away buggy flipped over during the third year of Bat's imposed banishment. Had Bat known of Trumball's demise, he would have returned to the Citizen Potawatomi Reservation before the expiration of the seven years that Trumball had ordered him gone.

Bat wasn't the only one with emotional tugs. After returning from a drive, Ricardo talked to Bat after breakfast. "Bat, I won't be going on anymore trail drives. I'll be settling down – my boys need me. They don't even know me when I return – as soon as they do, I have to leave."

"What'cha gonna do?" asked Bat.

"Probably get a job in the mines."

There were several moments of silence. Finally, Bat spoke up. "We've been chasin' steers up to Kansas for several years. You know the work on the Trail is gettin' slim. I've even heard that the Trail might be shuttin' down."

Ricardo looked at Bat and inquired, "You saying that you're quitting too."

"Yep! More importantly, I need to find my sons. When I go back, it'll be seven years since I seen them."

"When you leaving?"

"Next week."

******

When Bat got to the Cheyenne Agency Road, he turned east, the direction he wanted to take for the last seven years. After camping for the night and riding several miles, he said to Buck, "We'll be at the Arbuckle Wagon Road in one more mile and cross Little River." Just as he crossed the river, a stark reminder of the fears that had gripped him was seen on the west side of the road – the hanging tree – the twitching feet of the horse thieves. Instead of stopping at his cabin a short distance southeast, Bat spurred Buck into a gallop and sped on past the lane that led to it. Remembering the past horrific scene of death, he began to tremble and wanted to get as far away from the tree as possible.

Bat anxiously and hurriedly rode south toward the cabin where his sister, Kate, lived. On his way, he passed the cabin where his mother and father formerly lived. It was now occupied by old friends, John Anderson and his family, people who had moved from Kansas with him and several others,

As Bat cantered his horse past the Anderson home, John dropped the file that he was using to sharpen his plow blade and ran into his cabin.   He shouted to his wife who was candling eggs, "IT'S BAT – BAT'S ALIVE!" Together, they hurried to the front door and watched Bat disappear down the hill west of their cabin. "He didn't even stop and say hello!" said a disappointed John to his wife.

A few miles farther to the southwest, Bat slowly rode past the dugout where he and Mary once lived. He had painful memories of her death, and the loneliness he felt began to surface. As he passed what now was but a hole in the ground concealed by the remains of a collapsed roof, he looked ahead and saw his sister's cabin. It too had degrees of deterioration. The thought of *"Joseph must not be workin' very hard to keep the place up."* momentarily flashed through his mind. However, he was really thinking of a more important matter – a reunion with Frank and Will.

There was no one in the front yard. "HELLO!" he hollered. "ANYONE HOME?"

Kate soon walked around from behind the cabin where she was scrubbing the laundry. The wet dress she had just wrung out fell to the ground when she saw her brother. "Bat!" she cried. "I thought you must be dead!"

After embracing Bat for several minutes, she looked up at him and said, "You look tired and hungry!"

"I haven't eaten for two days – was hurryin' home to see Frank and Will," he responded but noticed that Kate looked down when he mentioned their names.

"Is that Buck?" she asked. "Put him in the pen with the other horses and come inside." Kate took Bat by the hand and steered him into the cabin's kitchen. "You need somethin' to eat, and we got a lot of talkin' to do – like where you've been?"

Bat didn't just eat – he shoveled his meal.

"Bat, I heard there was a hangin' of two horse thieves the day you left. Somehow, the marshal thought you might be involved but some of the posse said you weren't," said Kate.

"Yes. I was let go, but the marshal told me to leave and not come back for seven years."

"Marshal Trumball?"

"Yep. Ed Trumball. He made me watch the lynching – he nearly caught me a couple of years ago on the Chisholm Trail not too far west of here – probably would've hung me then."

"Trumball! He's dead – died in a buggy accident 'bout two or three years ago. Must've been right after he thought he might've seen you," said Kate. Seeing that Bat was thinking about Trumball's death, she added, "If you were on the Trail, you must've been trailin' cattle. Is that what you have been doing all these years?"

"Mostly – driftin' back and forth from Kansas to Mexico."

"Mexico?" interjected Kate with a surprised look on her face. "I heard you might be there, but I didn't know."

"Yes, I was in Mexico. I met a Mexican – Ricardo Pacheco – he lives not too far from our Potawatomi and Kickapoo friends down there. He once was married to a Potawatomi, Stephanie Ogee. Remember her from St. Mary's Mission?"

Kate thought for a few seconds. After recalling the woman, she said, "Yes, me and her are the same age. We learned sewing together."

"You were the same age? She got killed – murdered by a soldier!"

"Oh, dear!"

The mentioning of Stephanie being murdered brought several minutes of silence.

Finally, Kate said, "You must be here to see Frank and Will. They will be very surprised 'cause they think you're dead too. Right now, they're in the boardin' school up in Shawneetown – Catherine Regnier feeds 'em when they're not in school."

A look of disappointment spread across Bat's face as he stared into a cup of coffee. "I thought you and Joe were be carin' for 'em," he said.

"We were, but I kicked Joseph out 'bout three years after you left. He got to drinkin' and was rough on me. Shortly before I got rid of him, I had another baby, Louie. Things were hard – raisin' so many children. Sacred Heart – it's a mission east of here – opened up an orphanage when Louie was just a baby. I put Frank and Will in it – later Louie. When our father came back . . . ."

"Father came back? I thought he went back to Wamego after Mother died."

"Life wasn't too good for him there. He got remarried, but had the marriage annulled because she got to runnin' around. Besides that he got robbed too on his way to try gold prospectin'."

"Where's he at now?"

Kate looked down, and Bat sensed that something was wrong.

Very quietly she said, "Father died last month. We buried him next to Mother up by John Anderson's place."

Kate then turned her gaze back to Bat. She then tightened her lips, looked away, and said, "Frank, Will, and Louie all run away from the orphanage. They said the nuns were too harsh. Anyway, all three boys got sent up to the Agency and were put in the government school at Shawneetown. Frank and Will are foster children with the Regniers, but Louie comes home in the summer."

******

Two men rode up to where Frank and Will were playing marbles with two other boys during recess. "Mr. Bergeron, here are your boys," said the superintendent of the government school in Shawneetown as he pointed to ten-year old Frank and nine-year old Will. Will looked up and recognized the superintendent but not the other man. *"Why did he say 'Mr. Bergeron, here are your boys?"* he wondered in his young mind. Frank was so excited that he was winning the marble game that he didn't hear the superintendent say anything. For that matter, he hardly was aware that he and the other boys were being watched by two grownups.

Bat, while looking at his sons, reached backward into his saddle bag and pulled out the brown, hand-made, clay marble, a birthday present that his father had given to him nearly thirty years earlier. He looked at it and after a few moments, pitched it to the ground. It landed in midst of the other marbles. Frank quickly grabbed it and put it in his soiled trousers, but didn't even glance at it or the stranger who had thrown it down.

Signifying to the superintendent that he wanted to leave, Bat and the superintendent turned and rode away. Bat sadly and dejectedly thought to himself, *"They are my sons, yet I'm not their father – at least as far as they're concerned. They look healthy and probably are better off than if I were to get back into their lives."*

A short distance from the Indian marble game, the superintendent said to Bat, "They are here because they ran away from the Sacred Heart orphanage school." Bat didn't respond and left.

As the children were filing into the school building after recess, Will said to Frank, "Mr. Coates told the man that we were his boys."

Frank while fumbling with the marble in his pocket responded with a frown, "We can't be. Our father's dead."

21 – Black, Dirty Grease

Bat had met Hiram Young from Concordia, Kansas, at the stockyards outside Abilene after the last cattle drive that he and Ricardo made up the Chisholm Trail. Hiram was a buyer who represented the eastern markets for which the cattle would be shipped on the Topeka and Santa Fe Railroad. After agreeing to a deal, Ricardo, though disappointed in the price per head, turned to Bat and laughingly said, "At least we don't have to take any buffalo to Chicago like I did a few years ago. Yes, they are ornery critters!"

The deal that Ricardo made with Hiram was made as the two men draped their arms over the stockyard fence and looked at the herd. Afterward, they, with Bat tagging along, went into the Longhorn Saloon for Ricardo to collect his money. Hiram insisted that the payment be in U.S. dollars. At first, Ricardo resisted and told Hiram that Texas ranchers loathed "Yankee money" and wanted their money in gold. He finally took U.S. dollars from Hiram and said to Bat, "It's about time they put the war behind 'em."

The conversation among the three men turned to small talk. Numerous drinks were poured. After an hour, Hiram got up to leave. He looked at Ricardo and said, "Don't worry about paying for the drinks. I own this place. Good-day gentlemen. I need to leave so that I can catch the next train to Concordia if I am to get home before dark."

As he was leaving, he heard Bat mention the words of Bourbonnais Grove and Kankakee and stopped. He turned around and looked directly at Bat. I never put two and two together. You're a Bergeron, right?"

"Right."

"Some of the people moving into the Concordia area come from those places and know some of the Bergerons back there. How do you know about the area?"

"I used to live there," said Bat.

"Hmm, happen to know any Letourneaus?"

"My family and the Letourneaus are good friends."

"Tell you what," said Hiram as he held the door open, "if you are ever come up this way again and need a job, look me up!"

******

Bat slowly rode north. He had left his sons for the second time. Departure the first time was out of fear for his life. This time, he left on his own accord. *"Was I selfish?"* He was plagued by the question for several days as he headed for Kansas.

Instead of going back to Louisville, Kansas, where his sister, Matilda Lewis, and her husband, Wesley, lived, he rode to Abilene, Kansas. Like seven years before, he didn't want to explain to his family in Kansas why he had abandoned his sons.

The rationale that he used for going to Abilene also related to the prospects of finding work there, either in the local cattle business or on the railroad.

Cattle drives from Texas on the Chisholm Trail essentially were becoming non-existent. Bat thought, *"Ricardo was right."* He soon discovered that the cattle pens in Abilene were being disassembled and trotted on Buck over to the Topeka and Santa Fe Railroad to apply for work.

Apprehensively, Bat opened the door to the Railroad office where he saw hopeful applicants who were being interviewed. "Take a seat," said a balding fat man. "I'll be with you in a moment." The man took swig of bourbon from a bottle that he kept in his top, right desk drawer, belched, and turned around to see Bat. "We only got openings for gang workers – you know, layin' ties and rails and fixin' tracks."

Bat judged the man to be arrogant and left without filling out an application. More importantly, Bat didn't relish the idea of slinging a sledge hammer and performing other tasks involving hard labor in the hot sun of a Kansas summer. Years earlier, he had learned from the relatives of his late, Irish wife that work on the rail beds often can be very back breaking. Mounting Buck, his stalwart equine companion, he said "Maybe, I can prospect for gold in Colorado. As long as we're this close to Concordia, let's stop there and visit Hiram Young. He'll probably let us rest up at his place. I'll also ask him while we're there if I can file your hooves and nail some new shoes on you."

******

"Good afternoon, Mr. Young. Do you have a room for the night for a drifter?" asked Bat as he courteously tipped his hat while still astride Buck.

Hiram was cussing and trying to fix his McCormick Reaper. His hands were smeared with black, dirty grease. At first, Hiram only saw the legs of Buck. Then he looked up and saw Bat. Taking a cloth and wiping his hands, he started to shake hands with Bat and then pulled back when he saw that his hands were still filthy. While taking a kerchief to wipe the sweat off his forehead, he said, "Bat – Bat Bergeron! Mable – MABLE! Come and meet Mr. Bergeron! I met him in Abilene last year! Remember me talking about him?"

While Hiram was talking, Bat got off Buck and greeted Mrs. Young.

Hiram gestured at Bat and said, "I've got a room for you if you can fix this thing!" He gave the McCormick Reaper a swift kick as he talked. "I need to get it fixed in time to bring in my wheat. It's already starting to ripen."

"I'll try," said Bat. He immediately began to work on the malfunctioning reaper that had caused Hiram's consternation. In a few minutes, he stood up and said, "It's the gear that makes the sickle bar slide back and forth. It's got a missin' cog. If you can get a new gear, I'll put it in for you."

"How did you find the problem so soon? I thought you only knew how to drive steers," commented Hiram scratching his head.

"My father and some of his friends – back in Louisville – used to have one of these here things. They went together and got theirs after readin' 'bout the McCormick Reaper in the *Ohio Cultivator*. Anyway, I was taught how to use one – and fix it if need be."

"My son," lamented Hiram, "used to repair my equipment, but he went off to be educated at Kansas A & M. He's studying chemistry – he told me he don't want to work on the farm after he graduates – said he wants to go to Kansas City." After a long pause, Hiram looked at Bat and inquired, "If you're passing through, I reckon that you quit driving cattle and got another job lined up."

Bat, while wiping grease off his hands, said, "You're part right. I decided to stop workin' on the Chisholm Trail – work of drivin' beeves from Texas isn't so good anymore – you probably already know that – but I don't have a job."

"Wanna stay and help me? Like I said my son's away at college. Besides that, my hired hand quit yesterday. I could use some good help. Remember what I told you in Abilene last year about working for me?" Hiram continued enticing Bat to stay. "There's a little house out back where you can live. For a couple of days – at least – you can eat with me and Mable. After awhile – after you get settled – I figure that you'll want to fix your own meals." Glancing at his wife, he jabbered, "Ain't that so Mable?"

She smiled and nodded her head in agreement.

"I can start you off at twenty dollars a month. It ain't much – I know – but you will have a roof over your head. How about it?" asked Hiram almost in a pleading fashion.

22 – Wabash! Wabash!

Twelve-year old Will just returned from the Chisholm Trail. Because of his stature and size he had been assigned as a cook's helper on the chuck wagon instead of as a drover as he had hoped. Unfortunately, his Aunt Kate didn't know what to do with him when he came home. Because of his experience on the Trail, she assumed that he would be good at herding the sizeable cattle herd that she got in her divorce settlement from Joe.

"Will, want to help me? How `bout goin' out to watch my cattle for the next two weeks? They's quite a ways from here. I'm afraid the red wolves have been takin' some of the calves," said Kate as she puffed on her pipe.

Will felt he owed his aunt something. After all, she had raised him and his brother after their father left them at the Indian Agent's office.

"Sure!" answered Will. *"Finally,"* he thought, *"I'm old enough to help Auntie Kate with something important!"* In Will's haste to please his aunt, he forgot to take any food with him as he headed north to watch over his aunt's herd.

Two days later, hunger pains drove Will to gnaw the reins of the horse's bridle, but he was too timid to go back to Aunt Kate for help. He had been sent to a watch over a remote herd of cattle and that is what he intended to do. *"Auntie Kate might think I'm too young for the job,"* he rationalized. Still he realized that to survive he must get something to eat. "Uncle Johnny Whitehead lives not far from here," he said to himself. "Maybe he will give me somethin' to eat."

Uncle Johnny's wife, Abigail, was in the front yard pulling up a bucket of water when Will rode in.   Upon seeing her, Will forgot the formal way of addressing her and immediately asked, "Can I get something to eat?"

"Why of course!" she answered. "JOHNNY, COME OUT HERE!" she shouted.

When Johnny came out of his cabin and saw the condition of Will, he said with utmost concern, "Abigail – get the boy some food! As soon as Will's through eatin', I'm gonna take him up to Agency and see 'bout gettin' 'him some help!"

******

As soon as they entered the Superintendent's office Johnny said to Will, "Sit down on one of the chairs by the window." Turning to Doris, the Superintendent's secretary, he asked, "Do you know where his brother Frank is?"

Doris replied, "He should be in the school." Glancing at Will, she thought, "*So should he!*"

"Please see if Frank's there – if so – get him and bring him back to the office – and have him wait with Will over there. I might be in talking with the Agent when you get back. Hopefully, he will want to see the boys after we talk."

Doris soon returned. Frank was with her and had a look of apprehension on his face. "Sit down next to your brother. Mr. Whitehead said that the Superintendent might want to see to both of you."

Frank and Will sat almost motionless in their chairs. "What's this about," whispered Frank. "Don't know," answered Will in a hushed voice. "Just know that Uncle Johnny wants to get me some help – guess both of us."

After twenty minutes, the Superintendent's door opened. Johnny and the Superintendent walked out still talking to each other.

Will heard the Superintendent say, "White's – they'll be in good hands."

Uncle Johnny started smiling when the Superintendent turned to Frank and Will and said while motioning to them, "Come into my office. I've got something to tell you."

******

Frank and Will were jostled from their sleep when the train began blowing its whistle and the sound of steam hissed as brakes began squealing against the train's steel wheels.

"WABASH! WABASH!" loudly announced the conductor.

After a six-day journey by stage coach and train from the Indian Territory, Frank and Will finally arrived in Wabash, Indiana, to attend White's Indiana Institute of Manual Labor. The Superintendent of the Shawnee Agency originally had selected only four other Citizen Potawatomi to attend White's experimental educational program for American Indians, but John Whitehead had talked the Superintendent into adding Frank and Will to those already selected.

The boys felt strange while making the trip. They had heard from relatives and friends that a large group of Potawatomi had been forced out of northern Indiana and endured a "long walk" about a half century earlier. Nearly forty died along the way. Now, the six of them were being sent back to Indiana for their "own good."

Rather timidly, Frank and Will de-boarded their train. Each clutched a small battered suitcase containing their meager clothing, their only earthly possessions. As they stepped foot on the passenger platform, they heard the voice of White's superintendent, "Welcome to Wabash." Next to him stood a soft spoken blonde-haired woman, his wife. Both were in their late forties.

The superintendent of White's Institute of Manual Labor looked at the bewildered arrivals from Indian Territory and said while glancing back at his wife, "We each have a four-person buggy so choose one and hop in – don't crowd. We'll take you to the school. It's about a thirty minute ride southeast of town."

During the buggy ride to White's, Will scanned the fields that had been plowed in preparation for spring planting. He was intrigued by the black soil because he was used to the red earth of his reservation. In his naïve mind, he thought, *"How do they ever grow anything around here? That's the dirtiest dirt I've ever seen."*

*****

One year later, Frank, who had finished his program at Shawneetown before going to White's in northern Indiana, said to his younger brother as they were eating their breakfast of biscuits and gravy, "I'll be goin' on to Hampton this fall. Are you gonna come back here?"

Wrinkling his brow and sniffling, Will looked at Frank and responded with a question,"What's Hampton?"

Frank took another mouthful of his breakfast and said, "I'm talking about going to Hampton Institute. It's in Hampton, Virgina – far from here – near the Atlantic Ocean."

Taking a piece of bacon, Will began chewing and said, "If you're graduatin' and goin' way out to – where you say you'll be goin'? – oh, yeah – Hampton, I might come back here for a year or so, but after that I'll go stay on the Reservation."

"What are you gonna do on the Reservation?" asked Frank.

"I don't mean the Reservation itself. There's nothin' for me there." After a long pause, Will went on the say, "I'll be workin' several miles west of the Reservation. Mr. Taylor Fredrickson who runs the Katy Ranch over by Eldorado – west of Oklahoma City – once told me I could come and work for him whenever I grew up."

"Who's Fredrickson?"

" Ty Fredrickson? – He was the trail boss on one of the last drives on the Chisholm. I was the cook's helper on it."

23 – Where's He Going?

Bat tugged on the reins of the draft horse pulling the McCormick Reaper. Finally, he had completed cutting Hiram Young's golden brown wheat outside the growing town of Concordia, Kansas. He was covered with sweat. Sitting and taking a break, he thought of Frank and Will. "*I wonder what they're doing.*" Bat had no idea that their lives on the Citizen Potawatomi Reservation had been a struggle for them and that they now were in Indiana attending White's Indiana Institute of Manual Labor. Likewise, Frank and Will neither knew of their father's fearful encounter with Marshal Trumball nor that he was now working as a farm hand in Kansas. To them, their father was dead.

"It's a good crop!"

The voice startled Bat. Hiram, his boss, had walked up behind him when Bat had paused to rest and get a drink of water. Seemingly lost in his thoughts about Frank and Will and the death of his wife, Mary, Bat managed to tell Hiram what he had decided.

"After we get the wheat shocked and thrashed, I'm movin' on. I've been here for four years, and it's time for me to go."

"I knew that something was on your mind," said Hiram. "You've been restless ever since Buck died – not surprised, but hate to see you go. Where you going? Hope you don't mind me asking."

"Nope," replied Bat as he picked up a stem of wheat and began picking his teeth with it. "I'll probably head east for Louisville. My sister, Matilda, lives there, and I haven't seen her ever since she left the Reservation in the Indian Territory and moved back to Kansas. Actually, we saw each other for only a short time on the Reservation. My two half-

121

sisters, Archange and Olivie, also live somewhere around Louisville or Wamego – the last I knew."

"How you gonna get there now that you don't have a horse?"

"I'll catch a train in Concordia. It runs to Wamego where Mary and I were married. Louisville is just a short walk north."

Hiram noticed that Bat's eyes began to get watery when he mentioned Wamego and Mary. "Hope you don't mind me asking another question, but a couple of weeks ago you mentioned your sons. You never talked about them before. Are they with your sister, Matilda?"

The question was met by silence. Bat looked down and stared at the wheat stubble beneath his feet. Without even turning toward Hiram, Bat started walking the draft horse to the tack shed behind Young's house and said, "I'll start pickin' up the wheat bundles as soon as I get Ruby unharnessed and watered."

Hiram stood speechless. He sensed he had touched a very private part of Bat's life, a part Bat did not want to share.

*****

"Hiram! Isn't that Bat walking down the road?" asked Mable as she peered through her front window.

"Yep! He said last week that he's quitting. I happened to ask him about his sons, and he hasn't said much since."

"Where's he going?"

"Guess into town to catch the train to Wamego. He told me that he plans to visit his sister in Louisville – it's just north of Wamego – not very far north. From what I know, he's got sons there too."

24 – Matilda

"BAT!" shouted a familiar voice on the loading platform as Bat got off the train in Wamego. "I didn't ever expect to see you again! Everyone thinks that you got killed or somehow died!" Bat turned to his right and stared in disbelief. It was Mok-je-win who had married his half-sister, Archange.

"I thought you were living east of here!" said Bat.

"We were, but we moved into town. I got a baggage clerk job with the Santa Fe. Your father sold us his house when he went back to the Reservation down in the Indian Territory. Didn't he tell you?"

"Nope."

"Sorry to hear about Mary. I heard the sad news from Matilda."

"Thanks."

"Say, how's Frank and Will?"

Bat's stomach tightened when their names were mentioned. Instead of explaining to Mok-je-win about what had happened and what he had been doing since being run off the Citizen Potawatomi Reservation, Bat quickly changed the subject.

"I've come to visit my sisters and the rest of the family up here," said Bat. "I was pretty sure that I could see Matilda and Wesley, but didn't know if I could find you and Archange. Where's Olivie?"

"Olivie's a nun. She joined the convent at St. Mary's. A change came over her after Kah-dah-das was killed in the Civil War battle over at Westport."

"I remember she took his death pretty hard. Good thing they never had any children," responded Bat as he looked around and saw the changes that had taken place in

Wamego since he moved to the Citizen Potawatomi
Reservation in the Indian Territory.

"It's kinda late in the day – too late if you're walkin'
up to Louisville. Want to stay at my place tonight? I get off
work in about ten minutes if you don't mind waitin'. We can
walk home together. Archange will be surprised to see you."

Bat was both excited and apprehensive. Surely, the
matters of his life since moving to the new Reservation and
what had happened after he got accused of being a horse thief
would be discussed with Archange and Mok-je-win. The
worst he thought would be telling about the abandonment of
Frank and Will.

*****

"Let's just go quietly in the front door," whispered
Mok-je-win. "Archange's usually in the kitchen gettin'
supper ready." Mok-je-win slowly opened the door.
Together, he and Bat tiptoed into the house. As Mok-je-win
had hoped, Archange had her back turned. She was pulling
out a tray of freshly baked buns from the wood-burning oven.
"This is better than I thought it would be," thought Mok-je-
win. He impishly looked at Bat and waved him forward.
Standing behind Archange, Bat said, "Need some help, Sis?"

Archange quickly stood up upon hearing her brother's
voice, a voice that she had not heard for over a decade. She
turned around with the hot tray of buns in her hands.
Standing motionless, she mouthed, "Bat!"

"You'd better put them hot things down if you want a
hug," said Bat with a wide grin on his mustached face.

*****

"Mornin', Bat. Did you get a good night's sleep?"
chirped Archange as she got her three granddaughters ready
for school. "I've got some coffee and breakfast ready for
you before you go on up to see Matilda and Wesley in
Louisville. You'd better get filled up. Matilda is expectin' a
baby any day. Don't think Wesley is much good at cookin'

124

so don't expect much in the way of food when you see them – especially if Matilda has a new baby with her."

"How often do you see Matilda?" asked Bat.

"About once a month," answered Archange.   "I've offered to go help her when her baby comes so I'll get to visit you'all then."

Archange's mentioning of Matilda impending delivery caused Bat to reflect back on the anguish that Mary went through in the pangs of her labor that led to her death. *"At least,"* he thought while eating his breakfast, *"I'll see Matilda at a happy time."*

*****

During Bat's half-mile walk to Louisville, he reflected on the day his family and six other families had met in Louisville to begin their trip to the new reservation in the Indian Territory. *"That was about seventeen years ago,"* he thought. *"A lot of things have happened since then. It'll be good to see Matilda and Wesley again, but I can't imagine that she's still havin' babies – hope they'll understand why I left Frank and Will."*

As Bat entered the small town of Louisville, he soon recognized its streets. After all, Louisville essentially was the town in which he had grown up. At the age of twelve, he had tagged along after his father who helped lay out the town's streets and remembered the lots his father and mother once owned.

"From what I remember, Matilda and Wesley live in a frame house across from a church – on a corner not far from a river – on the east side of town," Bat said to himself.

Bat causally strolled along several blocks. Along the way, a couple in a one-horse buggy passed him. A grizzled man, lacking his front teeth, was driving. The woman beside him, who Bat surmised was the driver's wife, was fat and unkempt. *"They make an interesting couple,"* sarcastically and unashamedly thought Bat. As the couple passed by, the driver tipped his hat and waved. At the same time, the couple turned to get a better look at Bat and began animatedly talking to each other. Bat wondered, *"Do they recognize me?"*

One block east of the courthouse, which Bat noticed was abandoned, Bat recognized Matilda's house. It looked the same as time when he and Mary had stayed with Matilda and Wesley after leaving their small farm north of town.

A feeling of excitement swept over Bat as he got closer to the house. Then as Bat walked up the front walk path, he saw his brother-in-law, Wesley. *"Just like old times,"* Bat thought. Suddenly, Wesley's tear-stained face told Bat that something was wrong.

"Where's Matilda?" asked Bat nervously.

Wesley looked up. He first managed a feeble smile when he saw Bat and then gestured with his thumb toward the house.

Bat hurried past Wesley and into the house. As his eyes adjusted to the house's dimness, Bat made out the figures of two women. They were crying and trying to comfort each other. Behind them was a bedroom with its door slightly ajar. Bat ever so slowly opened the door and saw Matilda. Beside her was an infant. Neither Matilda nor her baby showed any signs of life.

Bat's head immediately dropped. After closing the bedroom door, he walked outside and sat down next to Wesley.

"When?" Bat asked.

"Five minutes ago."

25 – Fetch Your Clothes

Wesley let it be known within three weeks following Matilda's death that he wanted to sell his place. Bat meanwhile, at the request of Wesley, stayed to help his friend and brother-in-law.

Several years later when Bat walked out of the house with his mid-morning coffee, he saw Wesley talking with the two-some he had seen drive by in their buggy on the day he came into town. After their visit with Wesley, which was accompanied by a lot of hand waving and finger pointing at the house, the couple left.

Upon their departure, Wesley sought out Bat who had walked back into the house and said, "Bat, I've got a buyer."

"Who?"

"The couple who just left."

"Them?" asked Bat with a tone of skepticism.

"Don't worry," responded Wesley. "It's Jake. Remember him? He used to run the livery here in town."

Knowing that the man was Jake caused Bat to laugh.

"What you laughing about?" asked Wesley.

"My mother used to tell me stories about Jake, especially how he got his teeth knocked out by a travelin' boxer!"

*****

"Time to go," said Wesley who returned from a meeting with Jake and his wife, Gertrude.

"Go? When? Where?" asked Bat who was splitting firewood.

"Now! Fetch your clothes and get in the buggy. I just sold everything. All I need to do is get my own clothes. Get yours!"

"Now?

"Like I said, 'Now!' I'm leaving town now! If you want to come with me, get your clothes and get in. I figure that we can spend the night at Archange's place in Wamego and can do some planning there."

"Where we goin' after that?" asked Bat.

"Down to the new Reservation! Josie and Ivy already are there. I plan to stay with one of them – at least for a little while. They'll probably welcome you too – providing you don't get too ornery. They don't like cussing and drinking – something you do quite a bit of. I'll do some trading down there, and you need to find your sons."

*****

"HELLO!" hollered Wesley. "ANYBODY HOME?" Hearing and recognizing the voice of Wesley, Archange came out of kitchen wiping her hands on a dish towel.

"Just me and Mok-je-win – that is he'll be home any time now. My granddaughters went home for the weekend." Seeing Wesley and Bat standing behind him, Archange asked, "What's up with you two?"

"We're going down to the Reservation," said Wesley.

"When you goin'?" queried Archange.

"Tomorrow! Can we spend the night here?"

"Tomorrow? Sure, but why the rush?"

"I sold my house in Louisville today and decided there was no need to stay," answered Wesley.

"So you're takin' Bat with you?"

"Yes. I need someone to go with me, and he's going to help plan our trip. Besides he needs to find Frank and Will – I think."

Turning to Bat, Archange said, "Mok-je-win can't do nothin' to help figure out your family problems, but after he comes home and eats, I'm sure he'll have some ideas on how to go – that's if you want his advice."

*****

"Good meal," Wesley said to Archange. "Bat and me probably won't get one like it for some time once we start traveling."

Sliding his chair back, Mok-je-win said, "Archange told me that you're plannin' to ride down the Chisholm Trail. Goin' over to Topeka and headin' south 'til you come to the West Shawnee Trail – is the shortest way. Lots of our people have started goin' that way. Some even veer southeast when they get to the old Osage Mission and go clear over to Baxter Springs before headin' to Shawneetown."

"Why go clear to Baxter Springs?" asked Wesley.

"Good trails and water all the way," answered Mok-Je-Win sucking noisily and futilely on his pipe. "Archange, get me some hot embers from the stove."

Bat interjected, "Me and Wesley plan to go down the Chisholm. Havin' worked on it for several years drivin' cattle all the way up from Texas to Abilene, I know it good."

Mok-je-win laughed, "You're not goin' all the way to Texas."

Leaning over and playfully punching Mok-je-win, Bat said, "You know what I mean. Also, there's a shortcut from here to the Chisholm according to Wesley. There's no need to go all the way west to Abilene to get on it."

Finally getting his pipe lighted, Mok-je-win puffed on it, turned to Wesley, and asked, "How's that?"

"You cross the Kansas River on the ferry here at Wamego and head for Council Grove. Once you get to Council Grove, you then turn southwest. You'll eventually come to the Chisholm."

Mok-je-win nodded his head as if he understood and put down his pipe. "Do you know this area?" he asked.

"Bat and me used to be scouts at Fort Riley. It must've been shortly before you were stationed at Fort Row. Some of our missions were into the country around Council Grove. At the time, we did not know it as well as we should have – right Bat?" said Wesley whose eyes turned and focused on the left side of Bat's neck.

"Don't know if Archange ever told you, Mok-je-win, but I got shot when I was a scout and jumped by some renegade Pawnees. Me and Wesley were near Council Grove at the time. After I got shot off my horse, one of them tried to cut my throat – see this big scar?" Bat pointed to the scar under his left jaw line. "Wesley saved me from gettin' killed – not to mention from gettin' scalped," said Bat as he brushed the top of his head. The look on Bat's face gave Mok-je-win the impression that Bat was reliving the horrific moment of violence.

"There aren't any more Pawnees in the area," quickly added Wesley while looking at Bat and back to Mok-je-win.

The three men discussed matters and told stories for several hours. The subject of their talking first dealt with the way to travel to the new reservation in the Indian Territory, but drifted to trivial and family matters and finally back to the route of travel.

Late in the evening, Mok-je-win yawned and stretched. After getting up and stretching again, he went over to the stove and opened a burner lid. Rapping his pipe on the edge of the stove and loosening up his pipe's ashes, he said, while pouring them into the stove, "Seems to me that you've decided to go down the Chisholm. – Luke Kopp, my boss at the train depot, told to expect a big day tomorrow so I best get to bed. Please excuse me. I'll see you off in the mornin'."

26 – I'm Their Father

Bat and Wesley were an unlikely duo as they pulled their buggy up to the hitching post in front of the office at the Shawnee Indian Agency, a governmental unit that originally oversaw the affairs of the Citizen Potawatomi, the Absentee Shawnee, and the Sac and Fox; and now the Kickapoo. Bat's brown complexion and black hair contrasted with Wesley's pale skin and red hair.

The back seat of their buggy was filled with an assortment of suitcases and bags of clothing. Tucked here and there were the camping supplies they had used in making the trip down the Chisholm Trail. Trailing behind the buggy was Bat's new horse, a pinto mare that he had christened Annie.

"I hope the Indian Agent can tell us where to find Frank and Will," Bat said apprehensively. "The last time I saw them was when they were playin' marbles at school. It's the brick buildin' on the other side of the road. We passed it." Bat craned his neck in order to see the spot where he had last seen his sons. It's 'bout ten years since I saw 'em. I didn't stay very long when I did. One of them – Will, I think – glanced up at me."

Wesley looked over at Bat and asked, "What you thinking about?"

"Just wonderin' if they still got the marble I threw down."

"Marble? I'm more interested in helping you find your sons than worrying about a marble. Let's go inside and see if the Agent can help us."

Bat was partially out of the buggy when he hesitated, pulled back, and sat back down. A myriad of ambivalent thoughts flooded his mind.

"Wesley, when I left my boys eighteen years ago, the only thing here was a red sandstone building. Now look, white houses up on the hill, a brick school, this here office building, and somethin' being built across from the cabin where the Bourbonnais's live – at least they used to. There's even a little church over there."

Wesley, who was already out of the buggy and tying the buggy horse's reins to the hitching post, impatiently said, "You're stalling, Bat! Maybe you're afraid of what you'll find out! Let's go inside and take care of our business."

Bat disdainfully looked at Wesley and almost tripped and fell to the ground when he jumped out of the buggy.

*****

Bat and Wesley were confronted with a rather curt "May I help you?" when they walked into the Agency's main office building. Sitting before them was Gracie Green, a rather matronly-looking woman with a round face and graying hair. She had her back to Bat and Wesley when they entered the office building and didn't bother looking at them. In front of Gracie and on her desk was a black machine that Bat had never seen before.

Before either Bat or Wesley could answer the secretary's abrupt greeting, the Agency's Superintendent walked out of his office smiling and talking to Napoleon Penacore, a man who looked at Bat and seemed to recognize him.

After a double take, Napoleon exclaimed "Bat! Is that really you?"

Bat smiled broadly, shook hands with the man, and said, "Yep!"

"We've got a lot of explainin' to do, but I gotta go right now." Napoleon turned to the Superintendent and said, "Take good care of Bat and his friend!"

Hearing the exchanges, the secretary turned around, but before she could find out what Bat and Wesley wanted, the Superintendent already was escorting them into his office. "Oh!" he said to his guests. "Sorry if Gracie sounded rude today. She's a bit nervous and frustrated. She got one of them typewriters yesterday afternoon and is figuring it out."

Bat and Wesley were directed to sit in the straight-back chairs facing the Superintendent's desk. Once they were seated, the Superintendent asked, "What can I do for you?"

"Mainly me," Bat unhesitatingly responded,

The quickness in which Bat spoke momentarily surprised the Superintendent. Sensing that Bat was a man who wanted help, he leaned slightly forward asked, "What's your name? If I can help you, I will."

"Bat – I mean John B. Bergeron."

The Superintendent put on his reading glasses and reached for a ledger book that contained the names of the enrolled Citizen Potawatomi. After scanning the names for a few seconds, he looked up and said with a degree of hesitation – "I find the name of a John B. Bergeron, but there is a note beside the name that reads 'reported to be in Mexico.'"

"That's me. I used to be in Mexico," Bat said calmly.

With a questionable look, the Superintendent asked, "Any relation to Frank A. and William O. Bergeron?"

"Yes – I'm their father. I want to find them and hoped that you can tell me where they live."

"You've been gone a long time," commented the superintendent.

"Yes," said Bat who hung his head, in part to conceal his inner turmoil.

"Well, it isn't my business to know why you've been away for such a long time, but I can tell you where your sons live – at least where William lives. A few years ago, I sent both of them to school in Indiana. From time to time, I see William so I know he's around. Frank – Frank, I haven't seen for a couple of years, maybe three or four. Not seeing him doesn't mean he's not around. Perhaps if you find William, I'm sure he can tell you something about Frank."

The Superintendent turned to Wesley and said, "I hope that you didn't feel that I was ignoring you."

"Not at all. I'm Wesley Lewis. My daughters are Ivy and Josie. They live down by Wanette. Me and Bat plan to spend some time with 'em."

"Ivy and Josie Lewis? – They are fine ladies, Mr. Lewis." A smile spread over Wesley's face.

Turning back to Bat, the Superintendent said. "Mr. Bergeron."

"Yes," Bat attentively said

"William lives not too far south of Tecumseh. Since you have been gone a long time, you probably don't know where Tecumseh is. Go about four miles south, and you'll come to it. Check around down there. You shouldn't have any trouble finding him because a lot of people know him."

"Thank you, sir."

When Bat and Wesley left the Agency's office building and got back into their buggy, Wesley turned to Bat and said, "It's too late in the afternoon to start looking around for Will. Let's go straight to Josie's and Ivy's where we can spend the night. First thing in the morning, we can double back up to Tecumseh and start looking for Will."

"I agree. I've been gone a long time. Another day won't make any difference," muttered Bat.

27 – Get the Gun!

While scurrying about under a pecan tree, Ivy said, "Josie, grab the other end of the sheet and help me spread it out flat so we can catch the nuts.

"Where's the long pole for knocking down the pecans?" asked Josie.

"It's in the buckboard. Go fetch it while I climb up in the tree so I can shake the branches you won't be able to reach. With you knockin' and me shakin', we should clean the tree pretty good," responded Ivy.

Sitting in their buggy partially concealed by a clump of sumac which had lost their leaves earlier in the fall, Bat and Wesley were humored as they watched Wesley's daughters strip the now leafless pecan tree of its prized bounty.

"Have you seen enough?" Wesley chuckled. "Let's go help 'em," he said slapping the reins across the back of the buggy horse. As the buggy bounced along, Wesley turned to Bat and proudly said, "You've got some hard-working nieces."

Annie and the buggy horse spotted the draft horses hitched to the women's buckboard and simultaneously emitted loud whinnies. Ivy and Josie both heard the horses' calls and immediately stopped what they were doing.

"Where's the sound comin' from?" shouted Josie up to Ivy.

"From over by the sumac," answered Ivy.

From her vantage point high in the tree, Ivy was the first to see the buggy moving in her direction. She shielded her eyes against the setting sun to see if she could make out who was comin'. "JOSIE!" she shouted. "Get the gun!

Some men are coming. Wait! Wait! It's father! Somebody's with him, but I don't who."

The excitement and happiness of seeing their father soon vanished when Josie said, "We got your letter a couple of weeks after mother died. By the time it arrived, we realized that we couldn't do nothin'. Did you get our letter? We mailed it from Wanette."

"Yes. I got it. Sorry that I never wrote again," replied Wesley. "I was sort of . . . . you know."

Gesturing to Bat, Ivy stepped forward and spoke, "Did you and him come together? Father, you haven't introduced us."

Looking at his daughters and then at Bat, Wesley said, "My apologies – I was thinkin' that you knew each other – but that was long ago – when you and your mother came down here – before we all went back to Louisville. Anyway, this is your Uncle Bat."

"UNCLE BAT!" both of his nieces exclaimed simultaneously as they held their hands up to their mouths.

"I – we – all thought you were dead!" said Ivy.

"Well, I'm not. I came to . . . . ," Bat started to say but was interrupted by Wesley who said, "Let's get the pecans picked up before the sun sets. We can talk while we work – by the way anybody here wanting some guests for a few days?"

Ivy and Josie still could not believe that their Uncle Bat was alive and had come back. Strolling over to the buckboard with her apron full of pecans, Josie turned her head toward Bat so he could clearly hear her above the whistling wind and said, "You started to say why you've come back but Father cut you off. Want to tell me now?"

"I want to find my sons, Frank and Will," Bat replied.

"You mean Frank and Will are my cousins?"

"Yep!" replied Bat as he dumped a hatful of pecans into the bed of the buckboard.

"I never thought of it that way," said Josie. "I saw Will last weekend. He came to the Gilbert's barn dance –

had Willie Jones with him – people call them 'Will and Willie' – they're planning to get married from what I hear. If they do, I hope they stick together – both of them drink a lot. Come to think of it, I haven't seen Frank for some time. Will lives somewhere near Tecumseh. Maybe Frank does too, but like I said, I haven't seen him lately."

"Me and your father want to go back to Tecumseh tomorrow mornin' and look for 'em," said Bat as he plopped his hat back on his head and pulled up the collar of his jacket to block out the cold wind.

28 – Looking for the Bergeron Boys

Bat and Wesley looked throughout the morning for the whereabouts of Bat's sons. "What are you going to say to your sons if we find them?" asked Wesley.

"Don't know – don't have any idea," replied Bat as he pulled out and studied his hand-sketched map of the Tecumseh area. Mumbling as if to himself, Bat said, "We've stopped and talked to lots of people. They said they know Will but not Frank, but don't know where to find either of 'em."

"What'd you say," asked Wesley chucking to his buggy horse.

"Just talkin' to myself," answered a contemplating Bat. "We've spent nearly two hours lookin' southwest of Tecumseh. They gotta be around here somewhere 'cause all the people we talked to said that they've seen – at least Will – headin' north or south and the Agent told us Will's somewhere south of Tecumseh. If the people said every time they've seen Will he's headin' north or south, it must mean they've never seen him goin' east or west."

"What'cha getting at?" asked Wesley.

"Then he's gotta be southeast of town. If someone in that direction from Tecumseh tells us he's seen Will goin' east or west we'll know we're getting' close to where he lives so let's look east of the Arbuckle Wagon Road," answered Bat still studying his map.

Reaching for a sandwich that Josie had prepared, Wesley said, "I see what you mean!" With his mouth full, he added in a muffled voice, "Want something to eat?"

Coming up from the south on one of the red roads that had been put in since the Land Rush, Bat saw a rider on a dapple gray horse. "Hold up, Wesley. Perhaps he knows somethin'."

"Whoa," Wesley said to his buggy horse and pulled up and stopped at the intersection.

The rider seemed to be in no hurry for he slowly gaited his horse to the place where Bat and Wesley had stopped. Next to the side of the buggy where Bat sat, he brought his horse to a stop. Warily, the rider wearing a heavy jacket and brimmed leather hat scrutinized the strangers. First, his eyes fixed on Bat. Then, almost as if scripted, his gaze shifted to Wesley, to Annie, and back to Bat.

The young rider, while looking at the trailing horse wondered which stranger actually owned it. He was thinking about buying another one with the money he had saved while working at the Katy Ranch. To his disappointment, the dark-haired stranger simply asked him where the Bergeron boys lived rather than inquiring if he wanted to buy the pinto. Because the young rider had an appointment with the Superintendent of the Agency in Shawneetown, he simply turned slightly in his saddle, pointed with a gloved hand to a simple log cabin with a small barn and a few outbuildings located about a quarter of mile down the road, and rode off.

"Thanks," said Bat as the small rider continued on his way to the main road.

The rider tipped his hat as his way of saying, "You're welcome."

As Wesley was turning the buggy in the direction of the cabin, Bat said, "The young man mustn't be able to talk. He didn't say nothing."

The cabin didn't have a hitching post in front so Wesley tied the buggy horse to the only tree he saw in the yard, a post oak with a few brown leaves, the harbinger of the coming winter.

Together, Bat and Wesley walked to the door. Bat saw as he was knocking that the threshold was dirt, a tell-tale sign that the cabin's floor was dirt too. He knocked several times, but there was no answer. All he and Wesley heard was the whistling wind coming out of the northwest. "It's getting' colder, but I'm willin' to wait. At least we found out where they live," said Bat as he pulled up the collar of his coat and put on his gloves to keep warm.

Bat and Wesley sat down on some crates they found next to the cabin and started waiting.

"I'm glad this place faces east – at least we're out of the wind – sort of," said Bat.

Getting tired of sitting, Bat and Wesley strolled around to see what Bat's sons were up to. "They must eat pretty good," said Wesley. "Look at the size of the garden." "Yeah," added Bat. "They also got some hogs and chickens. Based on the dung I saw in the pen by the barn, there's gotta be some cattle around here – perhaps they're on the other side of the hill over there."

Bat and Wesley returned to the crates and resumed waiting. Several hours later, Wesley pulled out a plug of chewing tobacco and asked, "Want some, Bat?"

Bat started to bite off a chunk but stopped when he saw the rider on the gray dapple horse coming down the road and turn into the cabin's yard. Bat quickly stood up as the rider dismounted and slowly walked toward him and Wesley. He stopped a short distance from the two men. The guarded look on his face told Bat and Wesley that the young man standing before him wondered if they had come on business, but he didn't know what.

Bat was the first to speak up. He asked, "Are you one of the Bergeron boys?"

"Yes. Why?"

Bat and Wesley looked at each other and were speechless.

"I'm Will. What can I do for you?"

29 – Lady in the Buggy

Bat was sitting at the kitchen table when Josie asked, "Uncle Bat, do you want some more coffee?" Without verbally responding, Bat slid his cup across the table so Josie could refill it. As Josie was filling Bat's cup, Wesley came into the kitchen yawning and stretching.

"Morning, Josie. Morning, Bat."

Josie returned his greeting. Bat did not. He was deep in thought about seeing and recalling what Will said during their rather awkward reunion the previous afternoon.

While sipping his coffee, Bat looked up at Wesley and said, "Will didn't seem to be excited about seein' me. About the only thing we really found out is that Frank is not here. Will mentioned that he's goin' to college at Hampton or somethin' like that, but didn't tell us where the college is at."

"I also noticed that Will didn't he say too much about Frank. What caught my attention is that he said something about them getting allotments up north" said Wesley who was holding his cup of coffee and staring out the kitchen window. "Don't spill your coffee, Bat – I think I see Will coming – Yep! It's Will!"

"I'll get him!" said Josie hurrying to the front door.

When she saw Will, he was standing away from the door. "What's with you?" she asked. "Don't you know how to knock?"

Will laughed and said, "Of course I do. I was just lookin' at the black snake baskin' in the sun by your door."

"What snake?" asked Josie who jerked the door almost shut.

"It's gone now. It slithered off when it saw me and you started openin' your door. It's probably somewhere under your honeysuckle bush."

"I hear we're cousins," said Josie opening the door wider and looking for the snake.

"Yes, I met your father yesterday afternoon. I thought <u>my</u> father was dead but when I came home who should I see?"

"I heard all about it," said Josie with a broad smile on her face.

"Are they here now – my father and yours?"

"Yes, come on in. They're in the kitchen. Do you want some coffee?"

"Thank you."

Will didn't know if he should address his father as "father" or "Bat" so he simply said, "Good morning" to Bat and nodded his head to acknowledge the presence of Wesley and Ivy who had just come into the kitchen.

He finally turned to Bat and said, "Considerin' the surprise of seein' you and Uncle Wesley yesterday, I forgot two things that you should know. I said that Frank is away at college. He's in Virginia, but will be graduatin' next May and will be comin' back. Also, both of us will be movin' to our allotments next summer." Will then finished his coffee and while staring at the bottom of his cup in a distant fashion said, "Thanks, Josie. I've got to get back and dig up my carrots and sweet potatoes. The frost two days ago already killed their tops. Good-day every body."

Silence pervaded the kitchen when Will left. Finally, Wesley turned to Bat and asked, "What are your plans today?"

Bat shrugged his shoulders and then replied, "I need to go look at my cabin. It's up by Little River. We went by it when we came down here. I'll need to tell Jeb Davis and his family I'd like to move in next month. He turned to Josie and Ivy and said, "Providin' you can put me up that long." Gazing out the window and watching Will ride away, he said,

"I'll look the cabin over while I am there and see if it needs any fixin' up."

"Seeing that you'll be busy, me and the girls will go down to Wanette without you."

*****

When Bat got to his cabin on the hill overlooking Little River to the north, he was prepared to tell Jeb that he would be moving back into his cabin, but discovered that it was empty. It had been vacant for some time considering that chipmunks had taken up residence in it. *"I wonder when Jeb left? He still owes me money, but I'm more interested in havin' a place where Frank and Will can come – if they want to,"* he thought to himself.

Bat slowly went through his cabin and looked at it from the outside to see what work needed to be done on it, especially because colder weather was coming. Mentally, he determined: *"About two weeks of work here – the chinking repair I can do without any tools – just a bucket – will need some tools to repair the windows and door – maybe Kate – I want to visit her anyway – has the tools that I need."*

Bat spent an hour looking around the cabin and premises. Finding a spot on a small hill that shielded him from the cool breeze yet provided warmth because of the sun's position, he laid down. Thoughts of past events flashed though his mind: *"the death of Joseph back in Kansas – his still born twins – the tragic death of Mary – nearly getting hung along with the horse thieves – getting run off for seven years – not seeing my sons for so long."*

He snapped out of his depressive thoughts when Annie snorted. "Well Annie, it's time to turn things around," he said as he stood up and brushed fallen oak leaves off his trousers. He then reached into one of his saddle bags and pulled out a small flask of whiskey. After taking a swig, he recapped the flask, put it back into the saddlebag, and rode west to the Arbuckle Wagon Road.

A buggy being pulled by a fast-moving Tennessee Trotter made him quickly rein in Annie when he reached the wagon road.

"Whoa," the lady in the buggy commanded when she saw Bat's pinto coming onto the wagon road. She jerked her horse's reins so hard that the horse reared.

Bat leaped off Annie and grabbed the buggy horse's bridle to get it under control and prevent a possible run-away. He turned to the driver and started to say "Your horse seems to be calm . . . ," but he stopped. The next word out of his mouth was "Madeline?"

She looked at him and asked in disbelief, "Bat?"

"Yes! Madeline LaFromboise?" he replied.

She laughed and said, "Yes, I'm Madeline. The last time I saw you, you were pickin' blackberries. I found out from my father, you got run off the Reservation for being suspected of stealin' horses. Is that true?"

"Being suspected – yes – stealin' – no."

"What'cha doing now?" Madeline asked.

"Just checkin' on my cabin," said Bat still holding onto Madeline's horse's bridle. "At the time you saw me last, I worked out a deal – sort of – with Jeb Davis to rent my place. He was hurt and couldn't work as I recall. Now that I'm back, I stopped by to pay him a visit and collect what he owes me, but he's gone – for some time it seems. Do you happen to know where he is?"

"Jeb – Jeb Davis died. He died several years ago. He never was able to work after he got hurt up in Kansas. Before his family moved out – I don't know where they are now – they scrapped together as much money as they could and gave it to my father. Mrs. Davis asked him to give it to you should he ever find you."

Madeline bowed and her voice lowered when she said, "Unfortunately, my father died three years ago from sickness. When I last saw him, he was in a real bad way so he gave me the rent money owed you and asked me to give it to you – should I ever see you. My husband, Dick Denton, got real sick and died too – two years ago this past June. I thought about using the money to help me and my family get through some rough times, but I said 'No! The money don't belong to me.'" While Madeline was talking to Bat, she reached into her purse and pulled out a small leather pouch with the letter "N" beaded on it. "I've been keepin' your money with me – hoped that I would see you some day." With a smile she opened the pouch and extended it to Bat. "Here," she said

Bat was grateful to get the money owed him, but what really caught his attention was the pouch. "Where did you get this?" he asked.

Madeline was not sure what Bat's question was and she replied, "Like I said, from my father."

"No! – Not the money! – The pouch!" Bat quickly responded as he softly caressed the pouch.

"The pouch?" responded Madeline growing baffled.

"Yes! – The pouch!" It was my mother's. Most of the time she kept it hidden."

Madeline surmised that the pouch meant more to Bat than the money in it and said, "Kate's your sister – right?"

"Yes."

"She gave it to me when I went down to visit her last month. Kate said she found it in her – your father's things after he passed away."

Bat realized that Madeline was looking at him in a strange way and changed the subject to get his mind off the pouch, "Do you visit Kate often?"

"Not really," answered Madeline pulling up her buggy blanket to keep warm. "When I saw her last, I was returnin' from havin' taken my daughter, Mary, to the Sacred Heart Mission. In fact, the reason I'm travelin' today was to see how Mary's doin'. That's how I happened to run into you. Well, I gotta go. I'm glad that I saw you and got your money to you."

"My pleasure," said Bat. Flustered he added, "Not the money, but meetin' you again. I hope that we can visit again someday." As Madeline was driving off, he shouted, "There's a barn dance at Anthony Gilbert's place this Saturday! Come on down if you can!"

Madeline turned with a smile on her face and waved. She had visited her daughter, Mary, at the Sacred Herart Mission now was headed to her place near Noble.

30 – Confrontation

Will waited in his buckboard beside the new Santa Fe Railroad Depot in Shawnee, Oklahoma Territory, for the train to arrive. Will had written a letter to Frank telling him about their father coming home and the circumstances in which they reunited. Frank later wrote back to Will from Hampton. He raised lots of questions about their father's long absence and asked Will to meet him with a buckboard on the second of June so he could get a ride to their cabin south of Tecumseh.

Frank had left for Hampton, Virginia, five years earlier with one suitcase barely filled with clothes. He was returning with three suit cases filled not only with clothes, but the books that he had acquired during his study of agriculture. When Frank arrived at Hampton, he was deemed not to be of good character. This was proven when he was thrown into Hampton Institute's jail for drunkenness. Now, he was returning as a respected college graduate knowing the latest methods of farming.

"FRANK, FRANK! I'm over here," Will hollered when he saw Frank step off the passenger car amidst a cloud of hissing steam coming from the train's under carriage. Frank nodded his head when he saw Will and walked over to where he was waiting. True to their reserved nature, the two brothers did not hug each other, but merely shook hands.

"Who's this pretty lady with you?" Frank asked with a grin as he winked at Will.

"Frank, this Willie," proudly said Will as he gestured to her. "We are goin' to get married next week!"

"Your names go together – Will and Willie!"

"Frank, you are not the first person to call us that."

147

Both brothers laughed and the other passengers on the platform looked around to see what was funny.

"Frank," stopped Will, "you should know that since I wrote to you, father got remarried – we have a stepmother."

"Who?" asked Frank.

"Madeline Denton – she's the daughter of Joseph LaFromboise. Auntie Kate once talked 'bout him shortly before we were sent to White's. Remember?"

"How come they didn't come to meet me here – like you and Willie did?"

"They live clear down by Noble," answered Will as he kicked at the bricks on the passenger platform. "Father sold his place by Little River and moved in with Madeline. Somehow, I guess he plans to make a living on her eighty acres – he had one hundred sixty."

"Did you ever ask father why he abandoned us and took off?" asked Frank.

"Yes, the first time I saw him at our cabin south of Tecumseh, but he got real quiet when I asked and wouldn't say anything. I don't know if he was ashamed, but he almost seemed scared of somethin'."

"After I get settled in – may take awhile – I will go down and visit him – perhaps we can go together," said Frank in a way that told Will that he wasn't overly interested in seeing their father.

Sensing Frank's awkwardness in talking about their father, Will changed the subject. "We got eighty acre allotments, Frank, over east of here by Econtuchka. The land is good. As a matter of fact, I've already built a house on mine. Me and Willie will live there after we're married. I figure that you will build on yours sometime this summer."

"How close are our allotments?" asked Frank.

"Right beside each other. Mine is north of yours."

Frank looked at Willie and said with a twinkle in his eyes, "I'll start building as soon as I get a good wife." He playfully slapped Will on the shoulder and said, "Let's get loaded up and go."

*****

"Was it really you who threw down this marble when Will and I were playing at school up in Shawneetown?" asked Frank the first time he saw his father at Madeline's place.

"Yes," replied Bat looking away from Frank.

"Why you didn't stick around and take care of us?"

Bat furrowed his brow and wouldn't answer Frank's question.

Finally, Frank said, "I've carried this clay marble around with me ever since then. Will told me that it came from you, but I told him that it couldn't have come from you because I thought you were dead – at least that's what I always thought – until Will wrote to me. In my mind all these years, I thought the man with the school superintendent might have been you, but every time when such thoughts came to me, I dismissed the notion. You can have it back! I don't want it anymore!"

A look of hurt came across Bat's face as Frank roughly handed the marble to him. At the moment of the emotional confrontation, Madeline came to the door of the cabin and said, "If you two men want somethin' to eat you'd better come in. Supper's ready."

Frank silently turned from his father and went inside the cabin to join Madeline. Outside, Bat intently looked at the marble and then threw it into the weeds by his yard as if trying to erase past memories. He then walked to the side of the cabin and bent over by the chimney. There, he moved a red sandstone slab that concealed his whiskey flask.

31 – Surprise, Bliss and Tragedy

Will suggested to Frank upon his return from Hampton that he visit Ty Fredrickson of the Katy Ranch about becoming involved in the cattle business. The next time Will saw Frank, he inquired how his trip to the Katy Ranch went. Frank replied, "Mr. Fredrickson told me he needs a trained bookkeeper."

"What did you tell him? You've gone to college."

"I was honest – said that I had studied agriculture at Hampton – not bookkeeping. Still Mr. Fredrickson seemed interested," said Frank.

"How's that?"

"He told me to get some schooling in accounting and come back and talk," answered Frank.

"Any idea where you can go to study – accounting?"

Pulling up a stalk of grass, Frank said, "Yesterday, I did some checking at the Agency. The Superintendent suggested that I go to Haskell Institute up in Lawrence, Kansas, and study commerce."

*****

Frank received his commerce degree, which involved some bookkeeping, from Haskell and planned to revisit Mr. Frederickson. Instead, he pursued romantic desires and married Mona Brussard, a Citizen Potawatomi like himself. Unfortunately, Mona contracted tuberculosis and died. Her death left Frank with an infant daughter, Elta

Although depressed over the enormous responsibility of raising Elta and being unable to find permanent work, Frank finally thought, *"Maybe Will can give me some advice."* Speaking to Elta as if she understood him, he wrapped a blanket around her and said, "Let's go see if Mrs.

Weldfeldt can take care of you today. I'm going to see Will."

*****

"Afternoon, Willie. I need to see Will. Is he around?" asked Frank.

"He should be in the garden. Said he was gonna weed the okra and tomatoes. If you look out back, you'll find him. Say, Frank, when you gonna start buildin' a house on your allotment?"

Frank smiled, slightly shrugged his shoulders, and went to find Will without answering Willie. He had more immediate concerns on his mind than house building.

Will was not in the garden, but Frank found him in his shed sharpening a hoe. When Will saw his brother enter the shed, he matter of fact said, "Frank, nice to see you. Hand me the other hoe. It's right by the door where you're standing. You can use it to help me after I get it sharpened."

Frank's responded with a slight grin, "I'm not here to sweat!"

"What'cha here for then?"

"I can't find any good work. Got any ideas. Besides that, it's hard to look for any – especially taking care of Elta."

"Me and Willie talked 'bout you and Elta the other night and were wonderin' how things are goin'. Have you been back to see Ty Fredrickson over at the Katy?"

"No!"

"Bet he would hire you now that you know bookkeeping."

"How am I going to talk to Mr. Fredrickson? He's west of Oklahoma City. Elta and I live south of Tecumseh."

"Ever thought about movin' in with me and Willie? I know that Willie would be willing to care of Elta so you can travel. Besides, having Elta around would be good practice for her. She's gonna have a baby!"

*****

Frank's route to the Katy Ranch took him through the rapidly growing Oklahoma City. Because of the distance to the ranch, he had to get lodging, coming and going. Will soon became suspicious of Frank's growing frequencies of trips. Finally, Will came right out and inquired, "Frank, you must be doing really good in the cattle business or <u>is</u> there something else going on?"

Frank, taking off his hat and shedding his jacket, smiled and said to Will, "I met a beautiful woman at the Scissortail Hotel when I stayed there."

"I thought so! What's her name?"

"Lulu – Lulu Evans."

"Lulu Evans? Is her father Tom Evans – the fiddler – whistlin' Tom?" questioned Will.

"I don't know. She's never talked much about her family. All I know is that she comes from around Virden and that her mother is dead."

"Then she's gotta be Tom's daughter," said Will.

*****

Suddenly, Willie screamed while she was playing dominoes with Will and Frank. She clutched her stomach. Will grabbed her. Seeing fear and pain on Willie's face, he shouted, "FRANK!" "GO GET MRS. CLARKE! HURRY!"

In the few minutes it took Frank to get Mrs. Clarke, who lived across the road, Willie started to hemorrhage after delivering a still born. Nothing Mrs. Clarke tried could stop the profuse bleeding and prevent Willie from dying. The two brothers looked at each other, one covered with blood and the other breathing heavily.

*****

Six months after Willie's death, Frank returned from Oklahoma City and told Will, "Lulu and I are going to get married." In the same breath, he said, "Any chance we could both live here until I get my house built?" Will, who was eating at the time, slurped his soup and simply nodded his head to indicate "yes."

Will then looked up and asked, "Does she know about Elta?"

"Yes. Lulu said she would raise my little girl."

*****

The bliss that Lulu experienced during the first year of marriage to Frank became complicated.

Frank and Will had just returned from 'noodling' for catfish in the North Canadian River when there was a knock on the door. "I'LL GET IT," said Lulu. "I'LL LET YOU!" hollered Will. "Me and Frank still are cleaning the flatheads we pulled out of sunken logs!"

Standing before Lulu when she opened the door was her father, Tom, and her fifteen-year old sister, Maude, a shy girl who had been dragged around from barn dance to barn dance, any place where her father was asked to fiddle. There was a third person with them who Lulu immediately recognized, her seventeen-year old second cousin, Alice. Lulu was surprised because all of them lived a three-day ride west of Econtuchka, and she wasn't expecting them. "Come in," said Lulu as she held the door open with a concerned look on her face.

"Who's there?" asked Will as he and Frank were toweling their hands and entering the front room.

"My father and my baby sister – and my cousin, Alice."

"Can't stay only for a minute," said Lulu's father. Taking Maude by the hand and moving her forward, he said, "W-what I came by for is to ask you to take care of your sister."

"What's wrong?" implored Lulu.

"Nothin' really. You see me and Alice here got married. Some of our neighbors, especially her mother, don't think it's right – if you know what I mean." Turning to Alice and smiling, Tom said, "Anyway, we thought it best to leave home awhile – if you know what I mean."

Frank and Will couldn't believe what they were hearing. Frank recalled writing to one of his teachers at Hampton, *"Some of the people here are not very good examples of civilization."*

"How 'bout it? Can Maude stay here?" asked Tom almost begging Lulu to say yes.

"I-I-I guess so," stammered Lulu.

"Good! I'll get her things from the buggy. She don't have very much."

"What I meant," said Lulu to her father as he was walking to get Maude's clothes, "is that I'll have to ask Will."

Tom either didn't hear her or ignored what she said.

Frank looked at Will and said, "I think Maude is staying with us. Hope you don't mind."

*****

While closing the ceremony, the judge in Tecumseh belched. "Excuse me," he said. "I now pronounce you man and wife. William you may kiss your bride."

Maude was only sixteen, and her marriage to Will required consent. It came from Lulu who had become her guardian after their father dumped Maude off. She agreed to the marriage after Maude said, "If you don't give me your blessing and consent, he'll ruin me."

On the way back to their home near Econtuchka, Maude asked Will, "Do you think Lulu and Frank will be moving in their own house pretty soon? It's pretty crowded, especially with Elta runnin' and Willis crawlin' around."

Will glanced at Maude and said, "Next week – their house will be done.

"You've done most of the work on it," remarked Maude.

"When you get to know Frank better, you'll understand why," said Will with a grin.

"I'm worried about Lulu," said Maude. "She's havin' a lot of pain. I know she's pregnant, but she shouldn't be in pain all the time."

"She didn't have any trouble havin' Willis," said Will as he cracked the buggy whip over the head of Susie to hurry their buggy horse to hurry along.

Upon arriving at their house, they were met by Frank. He normally didn't show any emotion or any sense of being in a hurry. This time he quickly stopped the buggy. While holding up Lulu, he said with a worried tremor in his voice, "Don't unhitch Susie, I've got to get Lulu to Doc Mulhaney! Something's wrong! I've never seen her like this! She was doing the wash and seemed fine. Suddenly, she doubled over and started screaming! – Please watch the little ones!"

*****

Doctor Mulhaney came out of the examination room and sat down next to Frank who was sitting with his head in his hands. "Frank," said Doctor Mulhaney, "your wife has a serious problem. She's pregnant, but the baby is in the wrong place. It's in a tube above the womb."

"I don't understand," said Frank.

"Let me draw a picture for you so I can better explain what needs to be done – if you want to save Lulu," said Doctor Mulhaney as compassionately as he could.

*****

Maude anxiously kept looking out the north window for her sister and Frank to return from Econtuchka. It wasn't until nearly sunset that she saw a buggy. Then she saw only Frank. "WILL," she hollered, "here comes Frank, but Lulu's not with him! She must be in the hospital!"

Frank turned into the yard and slowly tied Susie's lead rope to the trunk of a nearby elm tree. When he came into the house, he looked at the newlyweds and with tears in his eyes said, "Lulu's gone." His voice almost was inaudible.

32 – Nanny

Bat strolled out to milk his cow in the little shed behind the log cabin he shared with Madeline. As he passed the chimney, he stopped, looked around, and removed the slab of red sandstone, uncovering his stash of alcohol. His drinking had become more and more of a problem, one that was affecting his marriage to Madeline. He was unaware she suspiciously had followed him out of their cabin.

"SO THAT'S WHERE YOU'VE BEEN HIDING IT!" yelled Madeline when she saw what Bat was doing. The tone and loudness of her voice made Bat cringe, and he fruitlessly laid the slab back down. "I've been trying to stop!" he pleaded, but her tirade continued. Bat responded with a loud and long stream of cursing.

Madeline's daughter, Mary, who had come home from the Sacred Heart Mission, southeast of Noble, was inside the cabin washing dishes when she heard the loud offensive and defensive vocal exchanges between her mother and step-father. Bat's mongrel dog woke up. It had been asleep basking in the sun, but it quickly slunk away to escape the loud and angry verbal fighting. Mary threw down her dish rag and rushed outside. "STOP IT!" she screamed at her mother and Bat. Her intrusion had little effect on the ongoing verbal war.

Mary was at a loss of what to do when she caught sight of a buckboard approaching the cabin. "CALM DOWN! Mother, do you know the people who are coming?"

Madeline turned away from Bat to see who Mary had seen. Straining and shielding her eyes, she said, "It's Frank and his children, Elta and Willis – Bat, straighten yourself up! Frank and his children have come for a visit."

"Who's Frank?" asked Mary.

"Bat's son. He's the one who lost his wife about three years ago. He's now trying to raise the two children by himself. Remember me telling you about him?"

Mary, upon seeing Frank and the children and what her mother reminded her of began cycling ideas in her head. One idea became fixed: *"I think I've found an excuse not to go back to Sacred Heart."*

*****

The next morning after breakfast Frank said his good-byes and, as he turned onto the road, waved at his step-mother and father. The children quickly settled down in the buckboard's bed. Next to Frank sat a passenger who was not with him upon arrival – Mary. She had convinced Frank during the course of the evening, either by compassion or cunning seductiveness that he needed a housekeeper and the children were in need of a nanny.

The wheels of earlier wagons and buggies had made long ruts in the road because a heavy rain had fallen during the night, turning the road into a muddy quagmire. As Frank's buckboard bounced and jostled, Frank grew curious about Mary's obvious mixed heritage. He knew from his time at Hampton that Mary had some negroid ancestry.

"What do you know about your father?" he asked.

"Not too much," she answered. "I do know that he came from Nicodemus, Kentucky, and settled in Kansas – it's Nicodemus, Kansa, today. He and the others would've starved or frozen to death if it hadn't been for the kindness of a group of Potawatomi men who passed through after hunting buffalo. It's strange – I sometimes think of the Potawatomi as being some other people – but I'm part of us – anyway, he eventually come down to Noble – that's where he met my mother. He died several years ago."

"You know more than what you let on," said Frank. "All I know about my father is that he came from around Louisville, Kansas, moved down here, and abandoned me and my brother about the time my mother died – she died in childbirth – so did the twins she was carrying. My father doesn't talk much."

"From what mother has told me, he lived a few years in Mexico and learned to speak Spanish. Did you ever hear that?"

"No."

*****

Two years later, Frank and Mary and Frank's children returned, not in a horse-drawn wagon, but in a Model-T Ford. The biggest news was when Frank informed Madeline that she no longer was his stepmother but his mother-in-law.

33 – Bring My Fiddle

Frank and Will were harnessing up their mules to cultivate their corn when Frank said, "Will, Elta's got TB."

Will stopped what he was doing, looked at Frank, and responded, "I know you've been worried about her spittin' up blood. Are you sure it's TB?"

"Yes," answered Frank while he putting blinders on one of his mules. "I took Elta down to the Sanitarium last week for an examination and found out yesterday from Dr. Engdahl."

"What can be done for her?" asked Will.

"I was told the best thing would be to take her to somewhere it's dry. As soon as we get the cultivating done, I'm going to the Agency and talk to the Superintendent. Maybe he can tell me if the Bureau has any jobs in Arizona or New Mexico that I can apply for."

Will remained silent. He then surprised Frank when he said, "Me and Maude have been talkin'. I'm gonna sell my allotment as soon as we get our crops in and go into Shawnee to find work."

Frank ducked under the neck of his mule and said, "I'm not selling my eighty acres! I want my land when I come back – if me and Mary and the children go away for awhile."

Will sensed he had said something that bothered Frank. It was not just Elta's plague. After a few minutes of silence he said, "If you find that you can go – whenever that be – I can work the land myself. I'll send you your share of the crop money if you need to leave before fall. If necessary, I also will get you a renter."

A week before Frank and his family were to leave for New Mexico where Frank was to assume a teaching position in Shiprock, Mary spotted Bat coming for one of his rare visits to see his sons.

Mary found Frank who was in the back shed and said, "Your father's coming. He'd better be sober this time! You know what he's like when he gets to drinkin'. I don't like for him to be around when he gets drunk. It's not good for the children – Maude thinks the same way as I do. You know what I'm talkin' about!"

"We won't see him again for some time, so let's be tolerant if he gets on one of his cussing binges," said Frank. He gently squeezed Mary's shoulders to assure her that he would handle the situation.

Mary folded her arms and went to warn Maude to prepare her for Bat's coming.

Much to everyone's relief, Bat didn't take one drink and was exceptionally cordial during his visit.

Before supper and chatting with his sons under the shade of a pecan tree, Will told Bat of his plans to sell his allotment and move into Shawnee in order to better support his family. Bat merely shrugged his shoulders and wagged his head sideways as he pondered what Will said. When Frank told him that he and his family were moving to New Mexico, he reacted much differently. He looked at Frank and asked, "Frank, if you got a fiddle, can I play it?" A look of hurt began showing on Bat's face.

"MARY!" shouted Frank. "Bring my fiddle out here!"

While the three men waited for Mary to bring the fiddle, Frank and Will glanced at the other as if each was thinking, *"What's he up to?"*

After Mary brought out the fiddle, Frank opened its case and handed the fiddle and bow to his father. For a moment, Frank thought, *"This is the only thing I got of my father's after he left me and Will – except the marble."* Will remained silent, but seemingly knew what Frank was thinking.

Recognizing the fiddle as once being his before he fled the Reservation, Bat tuned it up and carefully placed the instrument under his chin. He then started playing a song that he had learned from his father. In the middle of the last verse he stopped, looked at Frank, and asked, "Will I ever see you again?"

34 – The Egg

Bat jumped and shouted, "Watch out! The last one's really floppin' around." Madeline deftly side-stepped the headless chicken as she brought another unlucky feathered creature to Bat. Just as Bat brought up his axe, he caught sight of a rider who was turning into the lane leading to the cabin. Giving the chicken a reprieve, at least for the moment, Bat stopped what he was doing said, "Madeline – it's Will!"

Will swung out of his saddle and stood looking at Bat who had wiped his hands and walked over to greet his son.

"Welcome, Will," said Bat. As he welcomed Will, he pulled Madeline forward and said, "This is Madeline. I know you've never met, but you've heard me talk 'bout her."

Madeline held out her hand to shake Will's hand, but he surprised her with a hug and said, "Hello, Mother."

"What brings you all this way from Shawnee?" asked Bat. "It's quite a ride – hope you aren't comin' with bad news. I know that you lost Gerald before you moved to Shawnee– nothin' else has happened – has it?"

"Naw," replied Will. "In fact, I'm practically your neighbor now."

"How's that?" Bat asked curiously.

"Me and Maude moved down near Wanette – we're on the Gilbert place. I'm back to farmin'."

"I thought you moved to Shawnee and were workin' there," said Bat.

"I did. After a couple of weeks, I got a job as a teamster for the milling company up there. It was a good job, but I got this here hernia and had to quit 'cause I no longer could lift those hundred pound bags of flour."

"I know that farmin' is hard work too so what kind of farmin' you doin'?" asked Bat.

"Oh, the usual stuff – cotton – stuff like that," replied Will.

"Shouldn't you be in the fields now? – Don't get me wrong. I'm glad to see you."

"We had a heavy rain last night so I decided to come up here and let you know where we are. While I'm here I was wondering' if you could tell me where mother and the twins were buried along Pond Creek?"

Will's query brought back one of the tragic memories Bat long had suppressed.

*****

Sitting atop Annie on a hill three months later overlooking his son's farm, Bat watched Will frolic with his children. *"I've missed a lot,"* he thought. When Bat got close, he could see that the children were barefoot and covered with sweat. He didn't know that they had stumbled across a ripe water melon in the cotton field where they had been working all day. It had been brought home as a reward and for eating. Most of the time, when a melon was found while picking the cotton, it was eaten on the spot. Will turned around at the sound of Annie's snort just as Bat was thinking, *"They're happy – I wish I was bringin' good news."*

"Well, hello Father," said Will. "I wasn't expectin' you." His greeting was punctured by the squeals of his children. "Excuse me, father – Griffith, get the younger children and get them washed up for supper. Blanch, tell your mother to set another plate – we've a guest."

After Will's children ran off for their scrubbing, Bat asked Will if they could talk in private.

"Sure," said Will who was concerned about what his father wanted. "Let's go sit in the shade. You might want to take your horse over to the horse tank first. She looks pretty worn out."

Bat did as his son suggested and then led his horse back to where Will was sitting on a chair that only had vestiges of paint still on it. Beside it was another chair of similar vintage.

"Sit down, Father. What's up?"

Rather unemotionally, Bat said, "Madeline died last week."

Will put his head down and said, "I'm sorry – do you want to spend the night with us so we can talk more after supper?"

Bat acknowledged the offer with a slight headshake.

Will said, "Put your horse in the barn. I'll tell Griffith to feed her." He then went into the house to talk to Maude.

Soon Bat heard Maude's voice coming from the house loudly asking, "WHAT DO YOU MEAN HE'S ALSO SPENDING THE NIGHT?" Bat had mixed thoughts at that point, *"Should I stay or go?"* He had learned a few years previously that Maude had very little use for him.

Later that night, Will asked his father, "What you gonna do?"

Bat looked into his cup of coffee and simply answered, "Work."

The next morning Will's daughter Josephine came in the backdoor of the little farmhouse with her lower lip stuck out. "What's wrong?" asked Maude. "I only got one egg," whimpered Josephine. "There should be more than that," said Will. "The chickens started layin' two weeks ago, and there are ten layers."

Awakened by the voices, Bat sauntered out from the bed that had been made for him in the pantry and said, "When's breakfast?"

"When? It's more like what?" groaned Will.

"Whadda you mean?" asked Bat scratching his head.

"I only found one egg in the hen house," remarked Josephine in her eleven-year old voice.

"Only one egg? That's all I need," said Bat.

"No! It's not for you. Maude is carryin' another child. She needs it!"

Looking at Will, Bat became upset and said, "What? I'm your father. I WANT THE EGG!"

As Maude hustled the children out of the kitchen so they wouldn't get caught in the developing argument, she heard Will sternly say, "Maude gets the egg!"

Bat then realized that his son was not going to let him have the egg and, in a rage, headed for the barn to get Annie. Along the way he muttered, "I hope my horse got fed! I don't want to come back here and not get treated right!" After Bat got Annie saddled, he reached into the saddle bag closest to him and pulled out his flask.

35 – Snowstorm

Their buckboard, loaded with supplies, a few groceries that they could not grow or raise, and the children, rumbled north out of Wanette. After several miles of vocal silence, except for the chatter and giggles of the children riding in the bed of the wagon, Maude said, "I don't like goin' into town on Saturday mornings."

"How come?" asked Will.

"There's too much ruckus!" answered Maude. "You were busy talkin' to Aunt Kate and Cousin Louie when two drunk fellas came tumbling out of a bar. They bumped into me and nearly knocked me down. Heard them laughin' about getting' a cub bear drunk – poor thing. Speaking of poor things – I don't see any sport in the dog and badger fights on Main Street!"

"Wadda we supposed to do?" answered Will. "Stay on the farm and starve! We need to come into town once in awhile. – Besides, a few years ago I might've been one of them drunks. – Good thing I got my life together at the arbor brush revival meetin'."

"You're right," responded Maude. "We both found the peace that my first grade teacher had. – Perhaps we could go into Wanette on Monday's – it'd be a lot quieter," said Maude.

As Maude was talking, Will realized that he had forgotten to water his team of horses before starting the trip home. Speaking to Griffith who was sitting between Maude and him and driving, he pointed and said, "Turn into the lane leading to Toupin's house."

"Why are we going up to see the Toupins?" asked Maude. "We saw them just a few days ago when they come by our place."

"We're not goin' for a visit. Even though it's cool today, our horses need water. Besides, I don't think any of the Toupins are home." As the team was driven to the water tank next to Toupin's barn, Will said, "Johnie go over to the well and pull up a bucket of water."

As Johnie turned the windlass on the drinking well and grabbed the bucket's handle, he grunted and asked, "What are we going to do with this water?"

"Get the ladle and pour water around the well.," said Will.

Johnie started doing as he was told.

"Let me do some!" clamored Helen.

"Be quiet," said Maude. "Johnie's almost done."

"That's right," said Will while looking to see how Johnie was doing. "When the Toupins get home, they'll see the tracks of the wagon and the horses, but when they see the circle you've made around the well they'll know that someone came just for water."

*****

Mr. Fundus, a crippled man came hobbling out of his house and waved for Will to stop as he and his family approached on their way home. Will was used to exchanging waves with his neighbor whenever he passed by, but he usually did not stop.

"Will, Mr. Fundus seems concerned about something!" said Maude.

"Yes, he does! Stop the team, Griffith!" said Will. The wagon stopped slightly beyond the lane to Mr. Fundus's farm so Will hopped off the wagon and went back to talk to his neighbor.

"Is something wrong – is Mrs. Fundus okay?" asked Will.

"She's just fine," said Mr. Fundus. "The reason I stopped you is to tell you that an old Indian man was trying to find you. From what I could tell, he was blind too – at least he don't seem to see very good."

"Thanks for tellin' me," said Will. "You'd better get back inside. It's getting cold. Do you need any help in carryin' in firewood?" Will looked at the sky and noticed the wind had shifted to the northeast as he was talking to Mr. Fundus and said, "Make sure you have plenty of wood by your fireplace. By the way the air feels, we could get some snow tonight. Are you sure that you don't need any help? Me and my boys can fill your wood box."

"Me and Thelma will be fine tonight. I've already got the wood box filled.

Seeing smoke rising from the chimney of Mr. Fundus's house, Will was assured that the old couple, who were his neighbors, would stay comfortably warm. "Okay," said Will. "I've got to get my family home."

As Will was climbing back onto the buckboard, Maude asked, "What did Mr. Fundus say?"

"He said that an old blind Indian man was trying to find me. It's gotta be my father, but I didn't know he was blind! It's been several years since I seen him. I think I should go find him and bring 'em home – at least for the comin' winter."

Maude rolled her eyes when she thought that Bat might be around. *"I hope he can behave himself and stay sober if he comes to live with us,"* she thought.

*****

Light was fading when Will and his family got home. As soon as Griffith and Will got the team of horses unhitched and unharnessed, Will saddled his riding horse, Pet, and walked her up to house where he tied her to a mimosa tree. He went inside his house and told Maude, "You and the children stay warm tonight. I've got to go and find my father. There still is enough light so I can see the tracks of his horse and tell what way he headed. If he headed north, most likely he headed home."

"What'cha gonna do if you find him?" asked Maude.

"I'll bring 'em back here," said Will while knowing that Maude didn't appreciate having his father around.

The wind already had picked up by the time Will began tracking his father.

*****

It was dark when Edith saw something sweep by the kitchen window. She got up from her chair and closely looked out. In a childish voice, she gleefully said "Snow! Snow!" Her older sister, Mary, left her warm spot in front of the fireplace and peered out to see for herself. Pressing her nose up against the glass, she said, "Edith's right! It is snowing!"

In order to better assess the weather herself, Maude opened the front door. What she saw alarmed her. Snow already had piled up by the door and wet, swirling snow pelted her face. A freakish snow storm had swept into the area. She quickly shut the door and muttered, "Oh, Lordee! Will's out in this stuff! He could freeze!" Realizing the danger that Will was in but not wanting to frighten her children, she said, "Get your mattresses and pull them up to the fireplace. I want you to be warm and cozy when your father comes back." She then sat down in her rocking chair with her three-year-old daughter, Alice, bundled in her arms. Her older children already had snuggled together in front of the fireplace. After looking down to make sure that her twins, Dee and Don, were covered, she began slowly rocking back and forth in her rocking chair while softly humming *Amazing Grace.*

*****

Will was determined to find his father even though he knew what weather conditions he might have to face in doing so. Fortunately, there was enough light when he set out on Pet for him to see that the tracks of his father's horse led north. "He's goin' back to his cabin up by Noble," said Will to himself. Soon, it was too dark to see any tracks. Even if it had been daylight, the falling snow would have obliterated them. *"I hope I'm right,"* Will thought.

By instinct and memory, Will trudged through the deepening snow and found Bat's cabin. By the time Will reached the cabin, the snow storm had abated, and Will saw a faint glow coming through the front window. Standing in front of the cabin but facing away from the wind was Annie. Giving out a sigh of relief, Will said, "Thank God! He's here!"

Will led Pet and Annie into the shed behind the cabin to get them out of the wind. Then, returning to the cabin and stomping the snow off his boots, he slowly opened the cabin door and went inside. Before him was his father, sitting at the kitchen table, before him was his flask – empty. A kerosene lamp illuminated the scene. It also was the only source of heat in the cabin.

"Good evenin', father," Will calmly said. "Mind if I get some wood burnin' in the fireplace? I'm a bit cold from ridin' up here."

Bat emitted a slight grunt.

Will squatted down and quickly got a fire started. Without moving away from the fireplace, he rapidly rubbed his hands together to warm them up. Standing up while shedding his wet and cold overcoat, he turned his back to the fire and said to his father, "Come mornin', we're ridin' back to my place where I can take care of you."

Will's words might as well as have been spoken to himself because the only sound he got in return was heavy breathing and snoring from his father, a slumped figure at the table.

*****

"When's Father comin' back?" asked Josephine the morning after the snow storm. Her voice revealed that she was worried. So were the rest of the children.

"Soon," replied Maude, but in her heart she had her own worries. *"God will bring him back."*

170

Late in the morning, Johnie looked out the window and saw two men riding up the lane. "FATHER'S HOME! FATHER'S HOME! He's got Grandfather with him!" he shouted.

Although the twins and the other younger children were oblivious to the situation, some of the older children and Maude looked out the window where Johnie had perched as the self-appointed lookout. Cheers filled the house and there was much relief. Maude also was relieved and thankful that Will was safe, but suddenly thought when she realized who was with her husband, *"I hope that me and Bat can get along."*

When Will and his father came into the house after taking care of their horses, they were met with smiles and hugs. Bat by nature was standoffish but tolerated the greetings. He could not see well because glaucoma had damaged his eyes. However, his nose told him that coffee was waiting for him.

"Thank you, Maude," he said kindly when she handed him a cup of hot coffee.

"Where's Will going?" inquired Bat upon realizing that his son was leaving the house.

"He'll be back in a few minutes," answered Maude as she picked up the breakfast dishes. "Can I get you a bowl of warm oatmeal?"

"That'd be might kind of you. I'm pretty hungry."

Will returned ten minutes later with a smile on his face. Stomping the snow off his boots, he said to his father, "I strung out a rope and tied it to the tree by the back door. I nailed the other end to the corner of the outhouse. You can use the rope as a guide when you have to go. By the way, there's somethin' I been wantin' to talk to you about."

"What's that?" replied Bat as he took a sip of coffee.

"You'll need to buy your own mattress if you want to stay here."

Bat's disposition immediately changed from one of gratitude to one of extreme displeasure.

Maude saw a look of coldness sweep across Bat's face and knew what was coming next. She quickly ushered the children into the next room, but they still heard Bat's loud cursing when Will told him the stipulation for staying.

After Bat calmed down, he asked, "Why?"

Will explained, "The cotton crop was poor this year, plus we're crowded. I can't ask the children to double up any more and can't afford to buy you a mattress. If you want one, you'll have to buy one."

Bat was not satisfied with his son's reasoning and erupted into another rage.

Maude caught Will's attention and motioned for him to come into the next room where she was so they could talk without Bat hearing them. "What are we gonna do with him?" she asked. "You know that with him being blind, he can't take of himself, and I don't want him around the children – not with his cussin' and drinkin' habits."

Will looked down at the floor and then at the ceiling. On one hand he felt a loyalty to his father, even though Bat once had abandoned him and Frank. At the same time, he knew that his family deserved a tranquil life. Finally, he said to Maude, I'll take him to Frank. Maybe he can take care of him."

Maude looked perplexed and said, "I thought Frank was in New Mexico."

"I heard he got back last week – the climate there wasn't helpin' Elta."

"If Frank's already back, when you gonna take your father up to his place?" asked Maude.

"Tomorrow – it's too late to ride up there now – tomorrow – first thing in the morning."

*****

Will and his father, Bat, rode steadily through the snow on their way to Frank's house. The snow's whiteness contrasted with the low, red sandstone out-croppings and portions of exposed red soil that bordered the road they were taking.   It was a beautiful sight, a beauty that differed from the reasons for making the trip.   Will had one thought, namely to convince Frank to care for their father.   Bat's thought was to find a place to stay without any restrictions.

Frank saw his brother and father coming and left the comfort of his house to greet them.

When Will saw Frank and got into the front yard, he said, "Welcome home. I heard that you came back."

"Thank you," replied Frank. "In your last letter, you said you left Shawnee and moved to the Gilbert place to take up farming. "How's it going?"

"Not so good – especially this year – the cotton crop was poor – we had a drought last summer," said Will.

"Sorry to hear that," said Frank.

The conversation then turned to a more serious matter. "Actually, I didn't come to talk 'bout farmin' but 'bout our father. Frank, can you take care of father – at least for the winter? He lost most of his eyesight when you were in New Mexico and can't fend for himself anymore." Frank already had noticed while Will was talking that his father was not looking around in his usual fashion but seemed to stare straight ahead. Frank was not even sure that his father could see him.

"Come inside where it's warmer. I'll have to check with Mary," said Frank.

When Frank told Mary about the reason why Will and his father had come, Mary gave Frank a head bob in the direction of the back porch. Frank knew that Mary wanted to speak privately. When they got out of earshot, Mary turned to Frank and looked him directly in the eye. She had one word, "NO!

36 – Haunting Memory

The snow from the storm that Will had faced in tracking Bat two nights before created unrelated problems for Frank as he, along with Will, drove back to his house from Norman. The slushy roads between Norman and Shawnee were filled with reddish potholes and countless mud puddles of the same color. As Frank and Will continued their drive, the road from Shawnee to the Econtuchka area became nearly impassable because of the mud. Frank's car, once a glossy black, was now a dull, reddish color. On the drive to Norman, the temperature was low enough so there was little melting. By evening, the temperature was higher, making for very poor road conditions.

Neither Frank nor Will spoke during the ride back to Frank's house. The only noise was that of the motor's 'put-put' sound coming from Frank's jalopy. The ride to Norman was different. It had been filled with the string of comments and questions coming from Bat. He was intrigued by Frank's automobile considering that he had never ridden in one before and couldn't see where he was going. Will, on the other hand, simply said, "I don't like these things because they won't stop when I say 'Whoa.'"

As Frank pulled into his driveway and turned off the headlights and engine, he grasped the steering wheel and sadly said, "What else could we have done with him? It wouldn't have worked out for him to stay in either of our homes."

Will was quiet. Finally he said, "No. It wouldn't have worked out – but father can't live alone – not with his blindness and age. I wish that we had gotten to know him. Did he ever tell you why he abandoned us? He never told me."

"No."

"It's like he gave us away," said Will forlornly looking out the side window.

"I know."

"It was sad to see Father sitting by himself when went to talk to Dr. Taber about why we wanted to commit Father to the state's mental hospital," said Will. "I was puzzled when the doctor said our father seems to have repressed part of his life. The staff there should realize that father doesn't talk much – especially 'bout himself – though they might be on to something. It's still kinda funny that whenever they tried to get him to talk about his life, he wouldn't say anything."

"Do you think our father has dementia?" asked Frank.

"No. At least not in the way the doctor described it," answered Will. "He never forgets a thing. Both of us know he drinks too much, but his drinking hasn't affected his memory – as far as I know – I wonder what will happen over there when he gets a strong cravin'," remarked Will.

"They'll find out how belligerent he can be if he ever gets hold of a bottle," said Frank staring at the steering wheel.

"What do you suppose caused father to go blind?" asked Will.

"Don't know. The doctor said his staff would find out."

"Did you notice that he kept muttering to himself as we were leaving?"

Frank looked over at his brother and said, "I remember him saying something in Potawatomi, but I couldn't understand him. However, what caught my attention is that he seemed to keep repeating the same thing. Did you catch what he was saying?"

"I don't really know. – It sounded like twitching feet, twitching feet."

Made in the USA
San Bernardino, CA
11 February 2014